I0456891

Happy Birthday, Beth

A southern fiction series.

This series follows the tumultuous life of a southern woman named Elizabeth Benson.

Book I: *The Foundation*
Book II: *The Deception*
Book III: *The Reunion*

Please visit www.LBBradyBooks.com for ordering information.

About the Author

L.B. Brady is a southern woman, born and raised in northern Alabama in the late 1940s. Like most women in the sixties, she married shortly after high school and began raising her family. Four children later, when her youngest started kindergarten in 1989, L.B. Brady began working on a project. Little did she know this project would turn into the "Happy Birthday, Beth" series and span across the next 25+ years. She began writing and had almost finished one complete book, but life became busy and the book was put aside. After sitting on a shelf collecting dust for the over a decade, she decided to continue working. Shortly thereafter, the one book became two, then three, and now she is currently writing number four. Her large family, strong southern roots, and a lifetime of stories and influences from growing up in the South yields an abundance of creativity that is evident in her writing.

Happy Birthday, Beth

"The Foundation"

By

L. B. Brady

Book I

Dedication

This story is dedicated to my four children,

Kelly, Russell, Christopher and Pamela.

You have brought immeasurable joy and happiness into my life.

I am extremely proud of the successful adults you have all become.

I pray that your blessings will be many and your sorrows few.

All my love to you, now and for always.

- Mom

Acknowledgement

A very special thanks to my daughter, Pamela. Without her encouragement and continued faith and support in me, along with her expert knowledge of the world of technology, this project would probably have remained on the shelf collecting dust. You have made what seemed like an impossibility, possible. I love you and I thank you from the bottom of my heart for all that you do and have done for me.

Prologue

Thomas Benson frantically paced back and forth across the wooden living room floor of the shaggy old house that he and his family called home. As he listened to his wife's pain-induced screams coming from the bedroom, huge beads of sweat rolled down his worried face as he fought the urge to burst through the door that separated him from his wife, Marie, and their unborn child. Elizabeth Hartman, Marie's best friend, was in there with her and he knew there was nothing he could do but wait. It seemed like hours ago that he had sent his eight-year-old son, Kenneth, to get Dr. Michaels. Marie's labor had begun very early that morning and since the baby wasn't due for another six weeks, she had hoped it was only false labor and that the pain would eventually go away. Instead, as morning turned into afternoon, they had become increasingly worse and continued to intensify as evening, with its unforgiving heat and humidity, approached. Fearing that something might be wrong, she had asked Thomas to get Elizabeth. After Elizabeth arrived and saw Marie's condition, she told Thomas that it was time to send for the doctor.

Marie was very frail and had had a difficult time bringing Kenneth into the world. Since then, she had suffered three miscarriages. Dr. Michaels had been extremely concerned about this pregnancy from the very beginning and had put Marie on bed rest almost immediately.

"Hello, Thomas," Dr. Michaels said as he and Kenneth entered the living room. "How is Marie doing?" he asked with concern.

"I don't know, Dr. Mike," Thomas answered nervously, sweat still rolling down his face and his voice cracking. "She's been screaming an awful lot, Doc, so I know the pain must be terribly bad. You've gotta do something, Doc, please," Thomas begged as he tugged vigorously at Dr. Michael's arm.

"You know that I'll do everything I can, Thomas," Dr. Michaels said as he put a reassuring hand on Thomas's shoulder. "Now you and Kenneth go wait on the front porch and try to stay calm," he said. "Just pray and try not to worry. I know that's easier said than done and I'll send Elizabeth out to let you know how things are going," he added trying to ease Thomas's fear. "Hopefully, it won't take much longer.

I know Marie has to be completely exhausted by now."

Dr. Michaels didn't waste any more time and with his black bag in hand, quickly went straight into the bedroom. Once inside he found Marie lying on a soaking wet sheet, her hair clinging to her sweat drenched face, hands tightly gripped around each of the bedposts. Elizabeth was sitting in a straight chair next to the bed doing all she could to keep Marie wiped down with cool, damp cloths.

"How close are the pains," a very concerned doctor asked Elizabeth as he began examining Marie.

"They're about three minutes apart," Elizabeth answered as she continued to wipe the sweat from Marie's face, "and very strong but nothing's happening, doc. I fear something's terribly wrong."

After careful examination, Dr. Michaels found that Elizabeth's fears were confirmed. The baby was in a breech position and this was not good. He knew that both Marie and the baby could die but he tried to hide his concern from the two women as he spoke. "Marie, the baby is out of position," he explained emphatically, "and that's why you're having such a hard time," he added as he looked into her teary eyes. "I've got to turn the baby in order for you to deliver. Do you hear and understand me?" he asked as he gently wiped her face with the damp cloth.

Marie nodded silently for she was too tired and weak to speak.

"I want you to just keep holding onto the bedposts as tight as you can and scream all you want to and as loud as you want to," he explained fervently, "because this is going to hurt and you don't have to be brave for any of us."

As Dr. Michaels began to turn the baby, Marie's screams could be heard all the way to the front porch where Thomas and Kenneth waited impatiently. The sound of their loved one's screams was almost more than either of them could bear. Thomas had heard all he could take and was about to burst through the front door when Elizabeth came outside. She stayed just long enough to tell him what was happening then quickly went back inside. Once again Thomas paced, from one end of the porch to the other and then back again, fearing the worst but praying for the best. At this moment he wished with all his heart that Marie's pain would end soon.

Feeling helpless, Kenneth sat down on the porch and leaned up against the side of the house and picked at the chipping old paint with his fingers. Silently he prayed, as he covered his ears with his hands and tried to muffle the sound of his mother's terrible screams.

After what seemed like an eternity, a sweat-drenched Dr. Michaels pushed open the screened door and slowly walked out onto the porch, rubbing his hands on a wet towel. Kenneth jumped up from his seat against the wall and went to stand next to his father.

"Well, Thomas, it pleasures me to tell you that you have a beautiful baby daughter," he announced cheerfully while giving Thomas a pat on the shoulder. "She's awfully tiny, maybe five pounds I'd guess, but otherwise she seems to be just fine," he added with a smile.

Thomas was overjoyed at the news and a wide smile consumed his once worried face. "Did you hear that, Kenneth?" he asked overflowing with excitement. "It's a girl! I have a daughter and you have a little sister!"

"I was hoping for little brother but I guess a little sister is o.k.," Kenneth replied matter-of-factly but very relieved. "I'm just glad it's over, for Mama's sake," he added as he wiped sweat from his own small forehead.

"Dr. Mike, what about Marie? Is she all right?" Thomas asked anxiously waiting for his reply but almost afraid to hear what his answer might be.

"Well, Thomas, she's definitely been through hell and back and she's totally exhausted," Dr. Mike answered. "Right now what she needs most is rest and lots of it. It will probably be a couple of weeks, maybe even longer, before she's her old self again," he reassured. "You can go in now and see them if you'd like but just for a few minutes. More than anything, she needs rest right now," he added as he gently took Thomas by the arm and walked him to the front door.

Thomas didn't need much urging and ran through the front door. When he reached the bedroom, he came to an abrupt stop when he saw his beautiful Marie holding their tiny little daughter wrapped in a swaddling blanket. He slowly walked over and sat down on the side of the bed next to Marie. He bent over and softly kissed her on the forehead and gazed upon this most precious little gift she had just given him.

"She's the most beautiful thing I've ever seen," he said proudly, holding Marie's hand. "What are we going to name her?" he asked.

Marie looked over at her best friend who was sitting quietly in a chair by the window. Elizabeth had been there for her through the whole ordeal and Marie could tell that she, too, was exhausted. Her heart overflowed with love for this wonderful friend that God had blessed her with. "There's only one name that will suit this little one, Thomas, and that is Elizabeth," Marie whispered faintly, a huge smile covering her face.

"Then that's what it will be," Thomas concurred as he picked up the tiny, blanket wrapped bundle. Like any proud father would do, he held her close, kissed her tiny cheek, and whispered, "Happy Birthday, Beth."

July 15, 1956

Chapter One

The early morning dawned like a raging furnace over the Tennessee Valley region of northern Alabama where the Tennessee River snakes its way through hundreds of acres of fertile farmland. It wasn't unlike any other July morning in the south where cotton is "king," sweet iced tea is a staple, sunsets are God's paintings and family is the most important thing you have.

As the tiny pink and white blooms of the cotton plants stretched for the sizzling-hot summer sun, they slowly begin to make their showy appearance.

The fields were green with both cotton and corn this time of year but come fall, when the cotton bolls were full and open, the fields would be as white as new fallen snow.

In the winter, after the cotton had been picked and all the fields had been turned and plowed, the contrast between the red clay and dark loams and fields of green winter wheat added vivid dashes of color to the landscape, reminiscent of a beautiful, patchwork quilt. Not to be left out and rising up to boast their superiority, were the large cedar and pine-covered mountains of the Appalachian Mountain chain, which extended its fingertips down into this quiet river farm valley.

Summers were long and hot in the Deep South, beginning in early May and extending well into September. The temperature and the humidity waged a constant battle each day to see which one would dominate – creating a steamy, suffocating heat. The rains had already become scarce, which was good for the cotton crop, but even cotton had its limitations. If it didn't rain soon the crop would suffer extensive damage and the poor sharecroppers who farmed this river valley land would be on the receiving end of the devastating result. So was the plight of the Benson family.

"Beth, honey, wake up," Marie Benson said as she gently shook her daughter's shoulder. "It's time to get up. You know you have to get ready for church and breakfast is already on the table. Hurry, now, before the biscuits get cold! I just poured some fresh water in the basin so be sure and wash up before you get dressed."

Beth slowly sat up in the middle of her big feather bed and cocked her head to one side. Her sapphire blue eyes squinted from the bright sun shining through the thinly curtained window on the opposite wall of the small bedroom she shared with her parents. Sighing, she stretched her arms up over her head as high as she could reach, then wiped her wet, curly blonde hair from her forehead and neck. She loved her feather bed in the winter when it snuggled up around her and kept her warm, but on these long, hot summer nights, it seemed to only want to smother her.

"Oh, Mama, do I have to go to church today?" she protested flopping her arms down beside her on the bed in frustration. "It's awfully hot. I just know I will surely die!" she exclaimed with undeniable certainty.

Marie could hardly keep from laughing out loud and quickly turned her head so that Beth couldn't see. It wasn't easy but she finally managed to put on her serious face once again. "You know better than that Rachel Elizabeth Benson," she said with that ever-so-familiar ring of authority in her voice. Beth knew that voice very well. "The day will never come when it's too hot to go to church. Now you get up this instant, you hear me?"

"Yes, Mama," Beth replied reluctantly, a tiny pout on her lips.

Yes, Beth had known what the answer would be before she had even asked the question. In her short ten years on this earth, she had never missed a Sunday going to church. If the world didn't end on Saturday night, Marie Benson, being the good conservative Southern Baptist that she was, saw to it that her family was at the Calvary Baptist Church on Sunday morning.

It wasn't that Beth didn't like to go to church or that she didn't believe in God, quite the contrary. The Reverend Jenkins had put the fear of the Lord in her on more than one occasion with his "fire-and-brimstone" preaching. His voice would slowly become louder and louder and Beth would wait with great anticipation. Then, just when the entire congregation was on the edge of their seat, he would pound his fist on the podium with such force that Beth feared he would break every bone in his hand. Each time, she would jump at least a foot off the pew and a cold shiver would run down her spine leaving her feeling as if the Lord himself had entered her body. Despite the fact that she knew exactly what was going to happen, she was never able to guess the exact moment. The element of surprise was most important to the reverend and he would usually succeed several times during the same sermon. That's how he measured its effectiveness. It was just that on these scorching hot days, he seemed to go on and on, and those little cardboard fans with the small stick handle stapled to the back provided very little relief from the heat. They were always with the songbooks in the rack on the back of the pews, but no matter how hard you fanned, they couldn't cool an ice cube.

Still sitting in the middle of her bed, Beth studied her mother as she retrieved her one and only Sunday dress from the tiny closet. Marie was a small, frail woman and the hard life of being a sharecropper's wife had left its legacy, for she looked much older than her forty-five years. Her hair, dry from the summer sun, was mostly gray now with only a hint that it was once the color of sand. The years spent in the fields under the hot sun had dried and wrinkled her hands, not to mention her face. She had only gone to school through the eighth grade and had married Thomas Benson when she was sixteen. Ten years and several miscarriages later, Kenneth was born. However, despite the hard life, Marie had remained strong in her belief that the family was the nucleus around which love and life revolved and she had never once thought of leaving.

"Now you best be hurrying, Beth, or we'll be late," Marie said as she laid Beth's dress across the foot of the bed and quickly left the room.

Reluctantly, Beth climbed out of her bed, putting her feet on the bare wood floor. Slowly she took off the thin, cotton nightgown and laid it on the bed. After washing in the basin of fresh water, she put on the blue flowered dress that her mother had lovingly made from a flour sack. As she turned to leave the room, she caught her reflection in the wood-framed beveled mirror that hung on the wall over the old tiger oak dresser. Both had once belonged to her deceased grandmother, Ruby Rachel Benson. Walking over to the dresser, she stood for a moment and stared at herself in the mirror. Slowly, she picked up the hairbrush and began brushing her long, natural curly hair. *Why do I have to have all these curls?* she thought, as she studied her small 4' 7" frame. *I'm not very pretty but I would be if I had a beautiful, store-bought dress all covered with lace and ruffles.* That was just another of Beth's many fantasies, fantasies that she knew would never come true because the reality of her life was all around her, everywhere she looked. They were poor and there was nothing she could do about it right now. The future was different and she could do something about that. Her first very important decision had already been made - she would never marry a sharecropper. Oh, she loved her father with all her heart, but she wanted more from life than what her mother had. Marie's days were long and hard and as Beth got older, she, too, had been given many more chores. She didn't mind the chores so much right now but this was definitely not the life she fantasized about in her dreams.

Suddenly, the sound of Marie's voice brought Beth back to the present. Realizing she'd better not waste any more time, she quickly took her morning constitutional to the outhouse then hurried into the kitchen.

"Good morning, Pa," Beth said happily after she had kissed her father on the cheek and sat down at the kitchen table next to her older brother, Kenneth.

Thomas smiled at his little girl. "Good morning to you, too, Doodlebug," he replied in his familiar deep voice.

"Kenneth, will you please pass me a biscuit?" Beth asked in her most polite, soft voice, "and some butter, too."

Kenneth, who was secretly Beth's hero, had graduated from high school in May. Lean and tall at 6'3", he also had those sapphire blue eyes and Marie's sandy-colored hair. He was quiet and easy-going and extremely smart. He desperately wanted to go to college and play basketball but in order to earn enough money, he would have to move to the city where he could get a job in the textile mill. However, that just wasn't possible right now and he would have to wait until next year. Since Thomas needed his help, Kenneth had agreed to stay through the fall until all the cotton was picked and taken to the gin.

While she buttered her biscuit, Beth looked curiously at her father, who was obviously in deep thought and quietly drinking his morning coffee. He was a tall, rugged-built man and his thick, curly brown hair had begun to display a few streaks of gray. His jaw was square and stern but he had a broad, kind smile. A strict but loving father, he was born the son of a sharecropper and having had no formal education, had remained to work on the same farm his father had worked before him. He worked non-stop from sunup to sunset, but for reasons she couldn't understand, the hard work hadn't left its mark on him like it had on her mother. For at the age of 50, Thomas was still an extremely handsome man.

After due consideration, Beth finally decided that her father was in a good mood this morning so she felt it safe to ask him about staying home from church. Being the youngest, and his little girl, she could sometimes wrap him around her little finger. Gathering her courage, she took a deep breath and bravely popped the question.

"Pa," she began in her sweetest, little-girl voice, "don't you think it's too hot to go to church today?" she asked. "You know how the Reverend Jenkins loves to preach and if he gets too long-winded, well . . . we'll all just surely suffocate to death right there in the pew!" she exclaimed with a great deal of convincing concern for her family's wellbeing. "You wouldn't want that to happen, would you?"

Quietly, and with hopeful anticipation, she waited for his reaction.

Thomas wasn't the least bit convinced, however, and slowly looked up at Beth over the rim of his coffee cup. Beth knew immediately that this wasn't going to be the answer she had hoped for.

"Rachel E-liz-a-beth," he said, slowly drawing out her name.

That did it! When he used her full name, emphasizing "Elizabeth," she knew there was no further need for discussion so she didn't say another word. It was when he called her "Doodlebug," the nickname he had given her when she was a toddler, that she knew she had him - hook, line and sinker. It was all too obvious to Beth and everyone else that today wasn't going to be that day.

"I'll hear no more about not going to church, young lady," Thomas declared. "After all these years, we haven't suffocated in church yet and I promise you that we won't today either," he said as he looked Beth squarely in the eyes. "Now eat your breakfast before it gets cold. It took a lot of hard work to put this food on the table and I won't see it wasted," he added adamantly.

"Yes, Pa," Beth said softly, her head hung low in defeat.

Kenneth, who had been silently watching this all too familiar scene unfold, couldn't contain his laughter any longer. "You try this every Sunday morning, squirt," he said as he reached over and rubbed the top of Beth's head, mussing her hair. "I can't for the life of me figure out why you keep on trying when you know it's not going to work."

Kenneth loved Beth unconditionally and she loved him but he did seem to get enormous pleasure out of teasing her. This annoyed Beth immensely and she sought out her mother to come to her rescue.

"Mama, make Kenneth leave me alone," she pleaded, a sulky pout on her face as she gave Kenneth a mean stare. "He's always picking on me and I'm gettin' tired of it and now he's gone and messed up my hair, too."

"Kenneth, you leave your sister alone and quit teasing her," Marie said sternly. "Besides, if we don't hurry and finish eating we'll surely be late for church," she added firmly.

Thomas, whose seemingly tough outer armor was actually easily melted, especially by Beth, had been watching his little girl closely and was no longer able to ignore the sad, little pout on her face. Kenneth's actions had certainly not helped the situation any either, leaving Beth looking very sad indeed. He was trying to think of a way to cheer her up when the idea suddenly came to him.

"Doodlebug," he began, a huge smile covering his face, "I believe you have a birthday coming up this Thursday. Number ten, isn't it?"

"Yes, Pa," Beth answered with excitement. "I sure will be ten years old!"

"Well, I have an idea I think you'll like," he added with a grin. "I'll make you a promise. Of course, this all depends on whether or not we suffocate in church this morning but on the off-chance that we don't, we'll celebrate your birthday a little early by going swimming this afternoon after dinner. Would you like that?" he asked trying extremely hard not to laugh out loud.

Beth's pout quickly turned into joyous jubilation. "Oh, Pa!" she shouted, unable to contain her excitement. "Do you really mean it?" she asked, almost falling from her chair. She loved to go swimming in the river. It was her most favorite thing to do in the summer.

"Yes, I really mean it," he answered nodding happily and laughing at his precious daughter's reaction.

"Can Roz and Richard come, too?" she asked. "Please, Pa."

Roslyn, whose middle name was Marie after Beth's mother, and Richard Hartman were Beth's best friends. They were twins, just three months older than Beth. They may not have been identical twins, but they had many of the same physical attributes. Both had chestnut brown hair and wide-set, jade-green eyes. However, their personalities differed tremendously. Roslyn was very outgoing and sometimes a little on the mischievous side. Richard had more of a shy, almost timid, nature. Girls weren't his favorite people, but Beth was different. Beth would always be different. She was more like a sister and he felt comfortable around her like he did around Roslyn. But that feeling would change in later years. They had spent their entire lives growing up together on the banks of the river. Beth had never called Roslyn by her name though. It had always been simply, "Roz."

"I'll ask Bill when I see him at church this morning," Thomas answered, pleased that he had put the sparkle back into his little girl's beautiful, blue eyes. "Now you'd better help your mother clean up the kitchen. We don't want to be late for church and make her mad at us, do we?" he asked.

"I'll hurry, Pa," Beth agreed as she pushed her chair away from the table. Then, scurrying around the tiny kitchen like a little field mouse, she quickly began clearing the table, which sat in the middle of the room on the bare wood floor. The wood burning stove and icebox occupied one wall of the small kitchen and a base cabinet to which the water pump was bolted sat on the wall that boasted the only window in the room. Indoor plumbing and electricity were luxuries the Benson family did not enjoy.

Soon, all was clean and the family climbed into their twelve year-old, black Chevy pick-up truck. With Kenneth sitting in the back and Beth sitting between her parents, off they went down the long, red dusty road to the Calvary Baptist Church.

Chapter Two

Just as her father had promised, and much to her delight, Beth didn't suffocate in church that morning. However, Sunday dinner was lasting longer than usual and she was becoming increasingly impatient as she listened to polite after-dinner conversation between the adults, who had continued to sit at the table long after they had finished eating. Marie had invited Reverend Jenkins to dinner and Beth had found it most difficult to be on her best behavior when she was about to roast from the heat. The wood-burning cook stove had made matters even worse by heating up the entire house, adding to everyone's discomfort. The heat hadn't seemed to bother the Reverend though, Beth thought. She had watched in utter disbelief as he quickly devoured three pieces of fried chicken before she could finish one small leg and giggled to herself as she thought how lucky they were that Kenneth had killed an extra big chicken.

Suddenly, Beth heard the Hartman's truck pull up outside and she stretched her neck to see out the window. "Roz and Richard are here!" she exclaimed excitedly. "May I please be excused, Mama?" she asked politely.

"Of course," Marie said with a smile. "You go ahead."

Barely able to contain her excitement, Beth jumped up from the kitchen table and ran through the living room like a bolt of lightning and threw open the front screen door, slamming it against the side of the house. Skipping steps, she jumped off the porch and didn't slow down until she reached the Hartman's truck, which was still moving.

Almost before Bill could get the truck stopped, Richard and Roz jumped over the side of the bed and onto the ground. The three youngsters were so excited they jumped up and down with joy, shouting and laughing.

"I can't wait to hit that water! Can you, Beth?" Richard asked while taking off his shirt. "I thought I was surely going to melt in church this morning."

"Me, too!" Beth agreed. "I tried to tell Pa this morning that it was too hot but he just wouldn't listen to me. I thought Reverend Jenkins was going to preach all day! Now I'm ready to go swimming," she said emphatically.

Beth looked toward the house and saw her father, mother, Kenneth and the Reverend standing on the front porch watching all the excitement.

"Can we go swimming now, Pa?" she asked, impatiently jumping up and down. "Don't you know, it's gettin' hotter by the minute?"

"O.K., go ahead on," he answered, waving his arm toward the river and laughing at their impatience. "Be sure and stay in the shallow water until we get there," he cautioned. *Oh, to be young again,* he thought.

"We will, Pa," Beth promised as she ran back into the house to change.

Thomas never let his children go swimming alone. That was one of his most important rules. The river was much too unpredictable with dangerously strong undercurrents. It could take a person under in the blink of an eye. Of course, he had taught both Kenneth and Beth how to swim and to respect the river, but he liked to be close just the same.

Roz and Richard could hardly contain themselves while Beth changed into her swimsuit. It didn't take her long and as they raced down the dirt road to the river, they left a thick cloud of dry, red dust in their wake.

Once all the commotion died down, Bill and Elizabeth joined the adults on the porch. They talked and laughed as they went back inside the house. After Marie cleared the dirty dishes from the table and had put them in the dishpan to soak, she fixed everyone a fresh glass of sweet, iced tea. Soon they were walking at a snail's pace down the road that led to the river, following the cloud of dust left by the children.

By the time the grown-ups reached the "swimming spot" (the place where the river bank made a small beach-like place to wade) Beth, Roz and Richard were already splashing in the shallow, muddy water. Marie spread a quilt out on the ground in the shade of one of the many large trees that lined the riverbank. Here they sat down and began to talk and enjoy the afternoon and their iced tea. The shade did little to stifle the heat but the soft breeze blowing off the water helped to cool the air somewhat. Kenneth, being considerably hot himself, decided to join the younger ones in the water and swam on past where they were splashing to get out of their way.

Beth's attention turned from Richard, whom she was happily splashing, to the group on the bank. They were talking and laughing and enjoying the wonderful afternoon. She wondered how life could be any better than this. She thought it strange though to hear the Reverend laughing. That was quite a reverse from what she was used to hearing. When she finally turned her attention back to splashing water on Richard, she noticed that Kenneth was nowhere in sight. She quickly looked back toward the bank to see if he was there but he wasn't. It hadn't been that long since she had last seen him. Suddenly, a fear welled inside her that she had never felt before and it scared her to the depths of her soul. Without warning, she began screaming at the top of her lungs.

"Kenneth! Kenneth! Where's Kenneth?" she cried. "Pa! Come quick, Pa! Kenneth's gone!" she screamed once again. "I don't see him anywhere!"

"He was swimming out there in the deeper water just a few minutes ago," Richard yelled as he pointed away from the river bank.

Frightened beyond belief at Beth's screams, Thomas looked up to see her frantically waving her arms and jumping up and down. He and Bill immediately jumped to their feet, spilling their tea all over the quilt. Without removing so much as a shoe, they ran into the river where Beth was standing. The

Reverend, being of advanced years, stopped at the edge and watched in horror as he silently said a prayer.

Fear-induced adrenaline shot through Thomas Benson's veins as his eyes searched every inch of the water for his son. He was gone! "Where did you last see him, Beth?" he asked, fear gripping his deep voice.

Crying and pointing further out into the river, Beth exclaimed, "Over there, Pa, where Richard said. He was over there just a minute ago!"

Beth had been watching the Reverend laughing and hadn't noticed that Kenneth had gotten so far out into the river. Thomas had told her to always keep an eye on the other person because the current could get them and they could disappear in a heartbeat. If anything happened to Kenneth it would be her fault and she would never forgive herself.

The three ten-year olds got out of the water and stood beside their mothers on the bank and watched helplessly as Thomas and Bill searched. They dove down into the murky water time and time again where Beth and Richard had pointed, each desperately hoping beyond hope that they could feel Kenneth. Heaven knew they couldn't see him. Their biggest fear was that the current might have already carried him down the river. Again and again they dove, coming up only long enough for air. Neither one was willing to give up until they found him.

Marie watched in horror as her husband valiantly searched for their son. It seemed to be taking too long and a fear came over her she had never known before, the fear that only a parent who had lost a child could possibly feel. Elizabeth, however, was feeling something entirely different- guilt, because she was grateful that it wasn't one of her own children.

"I found him! I found him!" shouted Bill as he pulled Kenneth up out of the water. Although exhausted and breathless himself, he managed to get a good hold on Kenneth and began swimming toward the bank.

Everyone watched breathlessly as the reverend helped Bill get Kenneth over to the quilt where they laid him down. There was no sign of life and as Marie knelt down beside them, Bill began giving him mouth-to-mouth resuscitation. It seemed like hours, but only seconds passed before Kenneth began to cough up water and breathe again. Marie was overwhelmed with relief and she held her son close to her bosom, rocking him back and forth like a baby, all the while saying over and over, "Thank you, Jesus! Thank you, Jesus!"

Unknown to everyone on the bank, the worst was yet to come. Their attention had been so focused on finding Kenneth and reviving him, they hadn't noticed Thomas's absence from the group. Beth was the first to miss her father. Her heart began to pound fiercely inside her chest, as though it were going to explode. Panic overtook her small body and she began to shake violently. Looking in all directions, she screamed, "PAAAA! PAAAA! WHERE'S MY PA? SOMEBODY HELP! I DON'T SEE HIM ANYWHERE!"

"Dear, Lord," Reverend Jenkins said as he began praying once again.

Bill jumped to his feet immediately and left Kenneth's side and without a second thought, ran back into the river. He had never felt such fear for he knew in his heart, it had already been too long. Thomas was probably gone by now. But as exhausted as he was, he searched and searched until he lay on the riverbank, he himself nearly drowned.

Hours later, Beth stood on the river's edge, her tiny body racked with grief. Bill and Elizabeth had taken a distraught Marie back to the house almost immediately. Reverend Jenkins had gone to call Dr. Michaels, the family doctor, and the county sheriff, Homer Akins. Kenneth had wanted to stay with Beth but she convinced him that he should be with their mother when the sheriff came. Everyone had tried to get Beth to go home, even Roslyn and Richard had pleaded with her, but all she wanted was just to be left alone.

An agonizing six hours slowly passed and as dusk settled over the valley, Beth stood motionless as she watched the boats of men search the river for her father's body. Most of those who volunteered to help knew Thomas and were farmers who also lived along the river. *Why did God take my Pa away from me?* she asked herself over and over again. She loved him so much and she needed him here with her. How was she going to live without him in her life? *Maybe it was my fault! Maybe God is punishing me because I didn't want to go to church this morning,* she thought. It was like a terrible nightmare and she wanted with all her heart to wake up but she couldn't. Her eyes, red and puffy from crying, burned and hurt. Her heart was now filled with hatred for this river that she once loved so much and she never wanted to come here again.

Headlights suddenly stole Beth's attention away from the river and she quickly turned and looked toward the house. A car had turned into her front yard and she began running as fast as she could. Once there, she jumped the steps and was on the porch. Throwing open the screen door, she came to an abrupt stop when she saw Bill sitting on the sofa next to her mother. A trembling came over her body that she couldn't control and Kenneth put his arm around her shoulder and held her close to him. A cold silence filled the room as Bill took Marie's hand in his and cleared his throat several times. Tears filled Beth's eyes once again as everyone waited anxiously for him to speak.

"Marie," Bill began slowly. "Thomas's body was found about four miles down the river," he said with a great degree of difficulty, his voice cracking and fighting back his own tears.

Whatever else Bill had to say from that point on didn't matter to Beth. Nothing else mattered now that she knew for sure that her father was really gone. She turned abruptly, pushing Kenneth's arm from her shoulder, and ran from the house crying hysterically.

The next few days were just a blur to Beth. It was as if she wasn't really there but somewhere else on the outside looking in. Thursday, the day of the funeral finally arrived, and it certainly wasn't the way Beth had hoped to spend her birthday. It just couldn't be helped, her mother had tried desperately to explain. Something to do with the funeral home's schedule. Afterwards, back at the house, people from the church and surrounding community came and went, bringing with them their food and sympathy. Beth really didn't want either one, but she tried to smile and say thank you because her Pa had taught her to always be polite, no matter what. Despite everyone's kindness though, she was glad when it was finally over and everyone had left.

It was then that she sat alone on the front porch looking out toward the river she once loved so much but now hated. All she could feel was this huge void her pa's death had left in her heart and she made herself a promise right there on the porch that day. She would never again love anyone as much as she had loved her Pa. For now, all she could do was try to draw comfort from the memories of the many happy times she had spent with her Pa, especially the evenings sitting on his lap in the big rocker. There on the front porch, they had rocked while watching beautiful sunsets. After the darkness came, hundreds of lightening bugs would fill the air blinking their tails on and off. That had always been their favorite time of the day. Even though Beth had all these wonderful memories of times spent with her father to carry with her for the rest of her life, she knew, without a doubt, that the hurt in her heart would never go away.

Chapter Three

Beth learned the true meaning of friendship during the next few months. She also learned the true meaning of hard work. Alongside her mother and the other wives, she learned to can vegetables from the garden and make jams and jellies from the fruit they gathered, mostly blackberries, grapes and peaches. The apples and pears wouldn't be ready until the fall. Every farmer, black or white, young or old, not only worked their own share of the cotton crop, but they all pitched in to help Kenneth in the fields. At the end of each day, Beth would bathe on the back porch in the washtub full of water heated by the day's sun, then fall into bed totally exhausted. There, in her private little world, she would cry herself to sleep, completely oblivious to the fact that her feather bed was secretly trying to smother her.

Money was practically non-existent to the sharecropper. Each family had an account at Cooter's Corner Grocery where they charged staples such as sugar, flour and corn meal along with other items they might need during the year. It was located about 3 miles from Beth's house at the crossroads that intersected with the main highway going into town, ten miles to the north. The landowner, Travis McDonald, then paid Cooter Willis, owner of the store. When the cotton was harvested and the shares were divided, each family would pay Mr. McDonald for what they charged at Cooter's. There was never much left for the poor sharecropper and the cycle would begin again for the coming year. So much depended upon the weather, too, and because of a lack of rain this year, it looked as if there would be fewer bales per acre, meaning less money for each of the tenant farmers. Mere survival was life in the South for the sharecropper.

School started back that fall and Beth wasn't at all happy about being in the 5th grade. Here it was, only September, and all she could think about was the two weeks that school would close when the cotton was ready to pick. Not that she was anxious to pick cotton, everyone who was old enough had to help get the cotton picked but for some reason, she just couldn't bring herself to like school the way she once had. It had only been about two months since her father's death and she missed him so much she just couldn't bring herself to like much of anything anymore.

The sun beat down on Beth as she kicked at the rocks along the side of the dirt road on this hot, humid Friday afternoon. It was two miles from the school to her house and she deliberately walked as slow as she possibly could. She could have ridden the school bus but she was in no hurry today for she knew that chores awaited her attention as soon as she got home.

Her mind wondered from school to chores and then, for some unknown reason, to her shoes. She hoped they would last until Kenneth was paid their share of the cotton money, but from the looks of them, she wasn't sure. She used to get a new pair when school started but not this year. This year she would have to wait. She did have one other "good" pair but she only got to wear them to church and on special occasions.

Lost in her thoughts, Beth was surprised when she looked up and saw that she was standing in her front yard. Taking a deep, cleansing breath she stared, for what seemed like an eternity, at the little wooden shack that was her home. She wished she could just turn around and run away but she knew she couldn't.

"Mama, I'm home," she announced as she opened the screened door and walked into the living room. After putting her book satchel on the sofa, she gave another sigh of discontent as she looked around the sparsely furnished living room.

"Beth, honey, what took you so long getting home today? It must be close to four-thirty," Marie called from the kitchen. "Didn't you ride the bus?"

"No ma'am. I decided to walk home instead. I guess for some reason I just wasn't in a hurry to get home today," Beth replied solemnly.

Marie appeared in the kitchen doorway wiping her wet hands on a dishtowel and silently observed a very sad looking Beth. Coping with her father's death had been very difficult for Beth but Marie had hoped that getting back in school with her friends would help. Obviously, it hadn't. Thomas's death had been difficult for Marie to accept, too, but she tried to make the best of their life as it was now. She could only pray that Beth would somehow find the strength she needed to get through this difficult time. That was all she knew to do, pray and trust God.

"Beth, honey, you need to go change out of your school clothes then go find Kenneth and tell him that supper will be ready in about an hour," Marie said. "Big Mose is helping him today down on that south ten acres by the river," she added. "Now hurry and get on back. I need you to peel the potatoes when you get back so they'll have time to cook."

"Yes, mama," Beth answered and went to her room and changed into some shorts and a t-shirt. "I'll be back as soon as I can," she said as she hit the back door running. It wasn't that far to the south ten acres so she ran most of the way, cutting through the fields, which she found out the hard way, wasn't a very good idea. The sharp, pointed edges of the cotton bolls were cutting her arms so she held them up over her head. The tractor finally came into view but it wasn't moving. *That's strange,* she thought. There was so much cotton left to defoliate, she wondered why they weren't working. As she got closer and closer to the tractor, she could hear what sounded like loud screams coming from that direction and her heart began to pound like a drum was beating inside her chest. The same way it had the day her Pa drowned. Someone had to be hurt, she thought, and paying no mind to the cuts on her arms, she quickened her pace.

A chilling fear swept over her once again when she realized that that someone could be Kenneth, just like that day at the river. A chilling fear raced through her veins at the thought of losing Kenneth.

He was her "big brother". He was so much a part of her life now and had always been there for her through good times and bad. When she was five years old he would let her sit it his lap and steer the truck when they would go to the store. He wasn't really old enough to drive either but their Pa would let him anyway. Memories of those wonderful, carefree days continued to fill her head as she ran faster and faster toward the tractor.

Beth wasn't prepared for what she found when she finally reached the tractor. Kenneth was lying on the ground covered with blood, moaning and half conscious. Big Mose was kneeling next to him.

Big Mose was another one of the sharecroppers who worked the McDonald farm. His real name was Mose Lemuel Jackson but everyone just called him "Big Mose" because of his size. He stood 6'5" tall and weighed around 280 pounds. No one around these parts messed with Big Mose, for any reason.

"Big Mose, what happened?" Beth asked breathlessly as she quickly knelt down on the ground beside them and put her hand on Big Mose's shoulder.

"I's don't rightly know, Miss Beth," Big Mose replied as he began to try and explain what had happened. "It all just happened so fast. I was just standing here by the truck waiting for Mr. Kenneth so we could fill the tanks again. When he pulled up and stopped, I guess he thought the tractor was out of gear but when he stood up to get off, it just leaped right out from under him and Mr. Kenneth, well, he just went flying off," he added motioning with his huge, muscular arms. "He hit the ground real hard, Miss Beth, and the tractor kept right on going," Big Mose continued almost out of breath and still motioning with his arms. "I was somehow able to jump up on the tractor but I couldn't get it stopped before it run over Mr. Kenneth's leg. It's hurt real bad, Miss Beth. It all happened so fast, there wasn't nothin' else I could do," he insisted as tears filled his big, brown eyes. "I'm so, so sorry."

"I know, Big Mose, I know," Beth answered trying to console him as best she could. "It wasn't your fault. It was just an accident. What we need right now is some help and I mean fast!" Beth exclaimed nervously, her heart still pounding.

Although scared at what she might see, Beth finally got up the nerve to look at Kenneth's leg. It was so mangled it almost made her sick to her stomach, but she knew she had to be strong for Kenneth's sake. *It's bleeding too much. I've got to do something to stop it,* she thought as she frantically looked around for a rag or something to use. She knew it was all up to her. Kenneth's life was in her hands and she had to act and act fast. Time was the enemy. "Big Mose, do you have a rag or something, anything that we can tie around Kenneth's leg?" she asked desperately looking around for something to use. "We've got to stop the bleeding before he bleeds to death," she shouted adamantly.

"All I got here is my shirt, Miss Beth. Will it work?" Big Mose said as he began to remove his shirt exposing muscles Beth had never seen before. With shaking hands, he handed it down to her.

It's sure big enough, Beth thought as she took the shirt and folded it as best she could and wrapped it tightly around Kenneth's entire leg. "Big Mose, I want you to press down on the shirt real hard with your hand and keep it there," Beth explained. "I'm going back home and tell Mama so she can come help you then I'll go get some help," she said excitedly her heart still pounding.

"I sure will, Miss Beth," Big Mose replied. "I won't let you down."

Beth trusted Big Mose completely. Knowing that Kenneth's life was in her hands, she took off running again as fast as her skinny, little legs would go. She took the road this time because she knew she could make better time than cutting through the fields. When she reached the house, she jumped the steps, flung open the screened back door and ran straight into the kitchen. Breathless, she came to an abrupt stop next to Marie, who was standing by the stove stirring a huge pot of pinto beans.

"Mama, Mama," Beth exclaimed breathlessly. "There's been a terrible accident with the tractor down in the field. Kenneth's leg's been hurt real bad! Big Mose is with him . . . . and you need to take him a blanket . . . and stay with them," she rambled barely able to talk. "I'm going to Cooter's store and use the phone. We need an ambulance here fast!"

Beth's declaration caught Marie completely by surprise and her face turned as white as a sheet and she was as motionless as a deer in headlights. Before she could utter a single word, Beth was out the door and once again running down the red, dirt road leaving a cloud of dust trailing behind her.

Kenneth was all Beth could think about as she ran toward Cooter's store. Was this her fault, too? Was God going to take him away from her, too? She kept asking Him why He was punishing her by bringing so much tragedy into her life. Was she a mean person? *Kenneth just has to be all right,* she kept telling herself. The warm wind blew in her face and washed the hot tears from her eyes and down her cheeks. The faster she ran, the harder she cried, as the possibility of losing Kenneth became an all too real possibility.

"Beth, what's the big hurry?" Bill asked as he slowed his truck down and pulled up alongside her, the red dust flying everywhere.

Beth was startled by the sound of Bill Hartman's voice and stopped dead in her tracks. Trying to catch her breath, she bent over and put her hands on her knees for a moment. She had been so deep in her thoughts, she had not even heard the rumbling sound of the truck's motor.

"I gotta to get to Cooter's . . . to use the phone," she said panting and wiping the sweat from her brow with the back of her hand. Kenneth's been hurt bad . . . and we need an ambulance fast!"

"Dear Lord," Bill exclaimed. "Get in, Beth," he said as he reached over and opened the door for her. Once Beth was inside, he took off for Cooter's as fast as he could, spinning tires and throwing dirt. "What in the world happened?" he asked, nervously waiting for her answer.

"I don't know exactly," Beth said, trying to catch her breath and quit crying at the same time. "Mama sent me to tell Kenneth when supper would be ready and I found them. All I know is what Big Mose told me," she continued to explain. "Kenneth and Big Mose were in that south ten acre field down by the river spraying and Big Mose said that the tractor must not have been in gear and when Kenneth stood up to get off, it moved and threw him on the ground, then somehow the tractor ran over his leg," Beth explained. "I heard Kenneth screaming before I even got there, so I know he's hurt real bad."

"Oh, my Lord," Bill said softly. *What else is going to happen to this family,* he thought as he continued the drive to Cooter's.

There were no more words left to say. Bill and Beth were quiet during the rest of the ride to Cooter's store. Bill knew how bad tractor accidents could be and he didn't want to worry Beth more than she already was. She had already been through so much for someone her age. What would Marie do if something happened to Kenneth, too, he wondered as the lights from Cooter's store finally came into view.

Beth didn't like Cooter Willis one little bit and she hated to have to go there. It was always dirty and he thought he could treat people any way he wanted to because his was the only store within ten miles of town. Not only was he old, ugly and skinny, his hair was long and thin and always looked like it needed washing. He smoked cigarettes and chewed tobacco. Even worse, he tried to hide his rotten, yellow teeth behind an un-kept mustache. He would even open packs of cigarettes and sell them to the young boys for 5 cents apiece and give them sips of his beer. Beth knew this because Kenneth had told her. The last time she was in there alone he had tried to get her to go into the back storeroom with him but she ran out the door like her pants were on fire and didn't slow down until she got home. When she told her pa what had happened, he was furious and told her to never go there alone again, and she never had. That was two years ago when she was only eight years old.

"We need to use the phone," Bill told Cooter once they were inside. "There's been an accident and we need an ambulance."

Beth stayed close to Bill, not wanting to make eye contact with Cooter if she could avoid it.

"Sure thing, Bill. I've got the number right here," Cooter said as he reached over on the counter next to the cash register and picked up a piece of paper. He handed it to Bill and gave Beth a wink and a smile.

Beth cringed all over and stood even closer to Bill as he walked over to the phone and made the call to the hospital. After giving them directions to the field, Bill thanked Cooter for the use of the phone and he and Beth got back into the truck and headed for the field. Beth was relieved when they were finally gone.

The ride to the field seemed to take forever but when they finally did arrive, Marie was sitting on the ground with Kenneth's head in her lap, the blanket covering him. Big Mose was still holding the shirt over the wound just like Beth had told him to do.

"Marie, how is he doing?" asked Bill impatiently as he knelt down beside her and put his hand on Kenneth's forehead.

"I'm not sure. He's passed out from the pain," she cried. "I'm afraid he's going into shock and I just don't know what else to do!"

"You're doing everything you can right now, Marie," Bill said. "The ambulance is on its way."

"I'm so glad to see you, Bill, but how did you find out that Kenneth was hurt?" she asked.

"I was on my way home from town and came upon Beth running down the road. She told me what happened while we were on our way to Cooter's," he began. "I called the ambulance as soon as we got there. Hopefully, they'll be here soon."

Beth felt helpless once more as she sat down on the ground beside her mother. Marie put her arm around her and gave her a comforting hug. They waited and waited. *Why doesn't that ambulance get here?* Beth was thinking when she faintly heard the siren wailing off in the distance. Soon the flashing red lights appeared and she watched anxiously as they got closer and closer and the siren got louder and louder.

Once the ambulance had stopped, the two men wasted no time getting Kenneth on the gurney and inside the opened back doors. Marie got in, too, but when Beth started to get in, Marie stopped her.

"No, Beth," her mother said. "I think it's best if you stay with Bill and Elizabeth for now. There's nothing you can do at the hospital. Besides, it'll be nice that you'll get to spend some time with Roslyn and Richard."

"But, Mama!" Beth protested emphatically. "I need to go with you!"

"No argument, young lady," Marie scolded. "That's just the way it has to be," she said simply. "We have to go now. I'll try to get word to you as soon as the doctor tells me something," she promised.

Beth knew her mother meant what she said so she reluctantly stepped back away from the ambulance, her head hung down in defeat. As soon as the attendant was inside, the doors were shut and the ambulance took off with siren blaring and lights flashing, leaving Beth standing in another cloud of thick, red dust. She felt that same familiar emptiness inside that she had felt once before.

Bill could see the concern on Beth's face and his heart went out to her. He was concerned, too, but thought it best to ease the seriousness of the situation. "What you say we go by your house and pick up a few things for you first," he said as he gently put his arm around her shoulder and guided her toward the truck. "I'll bet Aunt Liz probably has supper about ready. Are you hungry?" he asked trying to get Beth's mind off Kenneth.

"No, not really," Beth said sadly still wishing she could have gone with her mother to the hospital instead.

"Big Mose, would you like a ride home?" Bill asked. He knew Big Mose must have been feeling some sort of guilt because of the accident and felt terrible for him.

"Yes sir, Mr. Bill, that'd be just fine," he answered quietly. "I'll just get in the back."

"I'm sorry about your shirt, Big Mose," Beth apologized as they walked toward Bill's truck.

"Now don't you worry none 'bout that old shirt, Miss Beth," he replied. "I's just glad I's able to help and I hope Mr. Kenneth's gonna be o.k."

The sun was just beginning to set and it didn't disappoint. A glorious arrangement of reds and oranges displayed their reflection across the endless rows of cotton that stretched to the western horizon.

It reminded her again of her pa and past sunsets they had watched together. It was such a somber moment, as if God was telling her that everything would be all right. She had to believe that it would. A red sky at night was God's sign, she remembered as their silent ride continued. It wasn't far to Big Mose's house and Bill stopped the truck. Beth watched as Big Mose waved goodbye and walked up to the front porch. His house was just like the Hartman's house and her house. As a matter of fact, all of the sharecropper's houses were just alike. Beth was amazed that she had never realized that before this very night.

Elizabeth was just putting supper on the table and was surprised to see Beth walk in with Bill. Richard and Roslyn were surprised and excited to see Beth, but Beth was unresponsive and seemed very sad. They all looked at Bill for an explanation.

"There was a tractor accident this afternoon and Kenneth was hurt pretty bad," Bill said as he began to explain what had happened. "I happened upon Beth running down the road to Cooter's and she told me what had happened while we were on our way there to call an ambulance. His leg is hurt pretty bad, but that's all we know right now. Marie went with him to the hospital so Beth will be staying with us tonight," he added as he put his around Beth's shoulder and gave her a loving hug.

"I'm so sorry, Beth," Elizabeth said as she sat the plate of hot cornbread down on the table. "I'm sure he'll be just fine," she added trying to keep her tone light. She didn't want Beth to know just how concerned she really was. "We have to have faith and trust that God will see him through this ordeal. Now, let's all sit down so Bill can say the blessing," she added.

Everyone was quiet as they took their seat at the table and Bill said the blessing, adding a special prayer for Kenneth's survival and subsequent quick recovery. Richard and Roslyn were at a loss for words and silently said their own private prayer.

Beth wasn't sure just how she felt about God at this particular moment. After all, he had taken her father from her and now maybe her brother, too. She began to wonder how he could be this loving God she had heard about all her life.

After the food was passed around, everyone quietly began to eat. Elizabeth was the first to notice that Beth's plate was still empty. "Aren't you going to eat anything, honey," she asked with a mother's concern.

"No, thank you, Aunt Liz," Beth replied sadly. "I just don't feel like eating right now if that's all right."

"Maybe you'll feel more like eating something a little later," Marie suggested as she looked at Bill with a feeling of hopelessness.

"Yes, maybe later," Beth replied in a whisper looking down at the empty plate.

Beth never did eat anything and spent a very restless night, tossing and turning, half awake – half asleep. She hoped she had not kept Roslyn awake since they had had to share a bed.

The morning light brought news about Kenneth. Marie had called Cooter's store and he drove out to the Hartman's house to deliver the message in person. Bill took the piece of paper from Cooter and thanked him for bringing it to the house.

Reading Cooter's handwriting proved to be a bit difficult but Bill was finally able to decipher it and began to read. "Bill, the deep gash in Kenneth's leg took a lot of stitches. It is broken, too, and so is his left pelvic bone. The doctor said that if it hadn't been for Beth and Mose he might have bled to death. The good news is that he's going to be all right." Bill paused, gave Beth a smile and then continued to read the note. "He will be in the hospital for four to six weeks but his complete recovery will take several months. There will be no cotton picking for him this year. I would appreciate it if you could come to the hospital this afternoon and get me. Thank you for everything and tell Beth I love her. Marie."

Beth, along with the entire Hartman family, breathed a sigh of relief and she hoped the knot in her stomach would soon go away.

Bill went to the hospital that afternoon to get Marie. Beth wanted to go, but there was no need since she couldn't see Kenneth anyway. She was too young to go past the waiting room because the age limit was fourteen, and there was no way she could pass for a fourteen-year old. All she could do was anxiously wait for her mother to get home.

Marie was extremely tired when she and Bill arrived at the Hartman house. All she wanted to do was get Beth, go home, get a bath and go to bed. It had been an extremely long night and day. Elizabeth insisted they take some leftovers home with them for their supper, and Marie thanked her and Bill for the food and for seeing after Beth.

"It's time to go now, Beth," Marie said as she took the food from Elizabeth's hands. "Bill is going to drive us home. You can see Roslyn and Richard at church in the morning."

"Yes, Mama," Beth answered politely.

Beth didn't complain about going to church that next morning. She had been doing a lot of thinking since Kenneth's accident, and sought out Rev. Jenkins after the service was over. She hoped that he could answer some of her questions. She waited quietly outside until he was through shaking hands with everyone as they left the church.

"Rev. Jenkins, if you have time, I'd like to ask you a question?" she asked nervously playing with the long ribbon tied in her hair.

"Of course I have time, Beth," the reverend answered. "I'll do my best to answer your question," he added as he put a comforting arm around her shoulder. "Now, what's on your mind, young lady?"

Beth was extremely nervous about talking to the reverend. After all, he was the closest thing to God she knew. She rubbed her hands and fingers together and took a deep breath. "Reverend, does God punish you when you have bad thoughts?" she asked shyly.

Rev. Jenkins studied Beth for a moment, wondering what brought on this question. "No, honey, of course not. God doesn't punish us. He loves us," he began, trying to explain it in a way that Beth would understand. "Sometimes bad or difficult things happen in everyone's life. That's what makes us strong. It's also during these times that we have to have faith in God and trust that everything is in His hands and to remember His promise that He will never leave us. He is with us in the good times and the bad times. We may not always understand why certain things happen but that's what faith is all about. Does that answer your question?" he asked noticing the bewilderment on Beth's face.

"I think so, Reverend," Beth replied, still somewhat confused but feeling a little better and a little less guilty. "Thank you for explaining it to me. I'll see you next Sunday," she said as she ran off to find Marie.

Chapter Four

Kenneth spent four weeks in the hospital, and Marie went to visit him as often as she could. Beth was extremely excited when he finally got to come home and spent most of her free time helping Marie take care of him. Otherwise, she was doing chores and homework, leaving her with practically no time to spend with Roslyn and Richard.

Regardless of the situation, life went on one day at a time and they did the best they could. The other sharecroppers who lived and worked on the McDonald farm proved to be the best of friends and they all came together and worked the Benson's fields as well as their own. There wasn't much to do after the defoliant was sprayed but wait for the leaves to die and the cotton bolls to fully open, then the picking could begin.

With the arrival of October, the leaves on the trees displayed their brilliant and vibrant fall colors of red, orange and gold, and the cotton was ready to pick. It would be Beth's first year to pick cotton and Marie had made her a special cotton sack to use because the regular ones were much too large and heavy for her. As Beth watched her mother sew, she remembered the years when she was very small and would sit on the end of her mother's sack. Marie would drag it, and Beth, down the middle of two rows of cotton, picking both rows at the same time. The weight of the cotton and Beth would cause the strap to cut into her mother's shoulder, but she never once complained.

When she wasn't riding on the back of Marie's sack, Beth would play in the cotton wagon with some of the other kids. It was so much fun and the cotton was so soft. But those times were gone forever, just memories now, and she could never get them back. School would be out for two weeks and now, at the tender age of ten, Beth had to pull her own weight and pick the cotton just like everyone else.

Day after day they picked, from sunup until the darkness made it too difficult to see, stopping only for a thirty-minute noon lunch break. Each time the sacks were full, they were dragged back to the cotton wagon where they were weighed from a hanging scale and then emptied. When the wagon was full, the tractor pulled it to the gin where it was weighed and emptied. The empty wagon would then be brought back to the field and the routine would begin again. There were many wagons scattered across the hundreds of acres of cotton. This routine continued until all of the cotton was picked.

Despite the fact that the sharp points on the cotton bolls were sticking her fingers and making them bleed, Beth didn't cry. She was determined to do her part. Each night, after her bath, Marie would soak her tiny fingers in alcohol to help with the soreness. Afterwards, Beth would fall into her featherbed exhausted and not caring anymore if it did smother her during the night. It didn't, and at the crack of dawn every morning, she would drag herself out of bed and prepare to go back to the fields once again. She just kept picking. She wasn't fast but she was steady and did her best. Many times she thought she just couldn't work another day. However, she proved to be strong, just like her mother, and at the tender age of ten, Beth learned that with raw, gut courage and self-determination, you could accomplish whatever needed to be done. Beth made herself another promise there in the cotton field that year, too. No matter what she had to do, she would never be poor when she grew up.

Finally, and much to Beth's delight, the day came when there was no more cotton left to pick. However, when Mr. McDonald paid Kenneth their share, after deducting what they had charged at the store, there wasn't much to rejoice about. The drought had definitely hurt and the cotton production was lower than it had been in many years. As bad as the situation was, Kenneth knew that he had to keep his family together. The only way he knew to do that was to leave the farm life behind forever.

Thanksgiving was just around the corner, and Kenneth gathered his family around the kitchen table to tell them about the decision he had made concerning the future of the Benson family. He silently prayed that what he was about to do was the right thing. All hands were on the table, centered only by the oil lamp, patiently waiting to hear what Kenneth had to say. "Mama, since I'm the head of the house now," he began acting very mature for his young years, "I've made some decisions concerning our future. It's obvious that we can't live here anymore. Because of the accident, I can't do the work anymore, Beth is just a little girl, and you are just plain worn out, Mama. It's time for me to take over the responsibility of this family," he explained placing his hand softly on top of Marie's. "It's been hard for me but I've finally accepted the fact that, because of Pa's death and my accident, I will never be able to go to college or play basketball."

"Yes, Kenneth, I'm aware of all that and it breaks my heart to think of everything you've had to give up," Marie said lovingly, "and I've been wondering about what we're going to do, too. What do you have on your mind, son?" she asked.

Kenneth looked into the sad eyes of his frail mother whom he loved dearly. It was almost more than he could bare to see her so unhappy. She had never lived anywhere but here on this river and most of it in this very same house. He prayed that he was making the right decision, for all three of them. "Bill is going to drive me into town in the morning and I'm going to see about getting a job at the textile mill. If I'm hired, we can live in one of the houses in mill town. They're small, but not as small as this old place, and much nicer," he explained looking around the small kitchen. "There's indoor plumbing with hot and cold running water and electricity. The bathroom is inside and the stove is electric, too, so no more cutting wood. All you have to do is turn a knob. It will be so much easier for you there, Mama. I've put a lot of time and thought into this, and I promise I'm going to take care of you and Beth. What do you think?"

Kenneth asked with an unmistakable excitement and concern in his voice.

Kenneth was looking forward to starting a new life in town, away from the river. He had known for a long time that he never wanted to follow in his father's footsteps. He believed that his accident was God's way of showing him how to get his family out of this life of poverty and now it was up to him to do it. He believed that everything happens for a reason. This was the first step toward a better life for them, but as he sat looking into his mother's sweet, tired face, he couldn't find any excitement at all in her eyes. She had not smiled since Thomas's death. He had hoped this news would change that, but it hadn't.

Beth, on the other hand, was ecstatic. She had never been away from the river and was elated, and the mere thought of living in "the city" was reason to celebrate. She had only been to town a few times with her parents, but she was very small and didn't remember much about it. Now to think that she might actually live there was almost too much to even dream about. To imagine really living in a house with running water and electricity was almost impossible. Thoughts were running wild in her head about all the places she could see and the things she could do and the people she could meet when it suddenly dawned on her that she would have to leave Roslyn and Richard. They would no longer be just down the road. That would be a terribly hard, if not impossible, thing to do.

"Whatever you think we need to do, Kenneth," Marie answered. "It's like you said. You're the head of the house now so we'll do whatever you think is best for the family. You're still so young and to have to carry such a burden is a big responsibility. I'm very proud of you, son, for being so brave and wanting to try."

"Now don't you worry, Mama," Kenneth reassured Marie as he gave her a big hug before getting ready for bed. "We'll be just fine. You'll see."

Kenneth's trip to town the next day was a success and he returned home with the news that he had a job at the textile mill beginning the first Monday in December. That didn't give them much time to secure housing and get moved but the decision had been made, the wheels were in motion and the time to start a new life was just around the corner.

Thanksgiving came and went at the Benson house that year without much fanfare. They did manage to have a turkey and a few of the trimmings but with Thomas not being there to celebrate the holiday with them, it just wasn't the same. It was the first of many holidays they would have to celebrate without him and Beth was trying very hard to enjoy the day. Making matters worse, the Hartman's had driven to Birmingham to spend the holidays with Elizabeth's family so Beth would also be without their company this Thanksgiving.

Life went on and moving day arrived. It was a cold Saturday afternoon in December and with it arrived the threat of rain. With the help of the Hartman's and Big Mose's family, the last of the Benson's meager belongings was finally loaded into the back of the truck and covered with a tarp just as thunder could be heard rumbling in the distance.

Beth and Roslyn had been trying not to cry all morning but now that the dreaded time had come for Beth to leave, the tears began to stream uncontrollably from Roslyn's jade green eyes.

"Do you think we'll ever get to see each other again, Roz?" Beth asked as they hugged each other and she, too, began to cry.

"Sure we will, Beth!" Roslyn said with such certainty that it actually made Beth feel a little less sad. "We'll be best friends forever and I'll get to come and see you before you know it!" she added trying her best to put on a big smile even through the tears. "Daddy said he was going to try and get a job at the mill, too, so we can leave this place."

That made Beth dance with joy.

Richard quietly came up behind Beth and tapped her on the shoulder. "I'm going to miss you, too, you know," he said as Beth whirled around to face him. They hugged each other tightly and Beth kissed him on the cheek. No words were needed between them as they stood and smiled at each other.

"O.K., squirt," Kenneth called out as he was getting into the truck. "It's time to go. I think the thunder is getting louder and I'd like to get on the road now and ahead of this rain if we can," he explained.

Beth gave all the Hartman's another hug, said goodbye to the Jackson's and took her seat inside the truck between Kenneth and Marie. As they drove away, she turned to look out the rear window and watched as Roslyn and Richard waved goodbye. The tiny, wooden house, which had been Beth's only home, began to fade in the distance until it finally disappeared from sight completely as they crossed the huge, steel bridge that spanned the river. They were headed north the ten miles to town.

Gone were the young, carefree days when Beth and Roslyn played in the red dirt and made mud pies. Gone were the days when they chased butterflies through the fields of clover, hoping they wouldn't get a honeybee sting on the bottom of their foot, making it swell and itch. Gone were the days when she would sit on her father's lap in the big wooden rocker on the front porch and watch the beautiful sunsets across the river. Gone were the days of catching lightening bugs in mason jars. Gone were all the days of her first ten years.

She was leaving that part of her childhood on the river behind her forever, but she would always have her memories. The future was unknown and scary, but she knew she was ready for whatever it held in store for her because living on the river had made her strong. She had no idea what her life was going to be like in the unknown world of the city but she was extremely excited and looking forward to beginning her new adventure.

Beth's excitement grew with each mile as she watched the outside world unfold before her amazed eyes. As they entered the south part of town, the houses were large and unbelievably beautiful. Even in the dead of winter, the lawns were immaculately landscaped. She could only imagine what it would be like to live in such a grand house and have beautiful things and store bought clothes. Completely enthralled and totally mesmerized by the enormity of everything she saw, Beth was totally taken by surprise when the truck suddenly stopped, almost slamming her into the dashboard.

"Sorry 'bout that, squirt," Kenneth apologized.

"Why are we stopping, Kenneth?" she asked as she looked up at her handsome brother with a confused look on her face.

"Because we're here, squirt," he replied emphatically with a huge grin covering his lips. "We have arrived at our new home!"

"We're here already?" Beth asked her face glowing with excitement. "That sure didn't take long."

"Yep. This is it! This is the new home of the Benson family," Kenneth replied proudly as he opened the truck door and stepped out onto the concrete sidewalk.

Beth thought surely her eyes were deceiving her when she turned her head and looked out the window. They were parked in front of this monstrously large two-story house with two front doors and a long, covered front porch that reached across the entire front of the house.

"You're kidding with me, Kenneth," Beth laughed. "We could never live in anything as grand as this!"

"No, squirt. I'm not kidding," Kenneth answered with a smile. "The whole house isn't ours, though, that's why there are two front doors. It's actually two houses in one. They call it a duplex," he continued. "We'll be living in one side and another family lives in the other side. Most of the people who work at the mill live here in what is called the 'mill town'," Kenneth explained further as he motioned for Beth to get out of the truck.

Beth stepped out onto the sidewalk and slowly looked around. Sure enough, all the houses were just alike, except that they were painted different colors. "Mama, will you just look at this house! Can you believe this is where we're going to live?" Beth exclaimed. "Ain't it beautiful?" she asked with much enthusiasm, hoping that this would make her mother smile again.

"It's very nice, Beth," Marie answered softly. "I hope living here will make you and Kenneth happier than you were on the river."

Kenneth and Beth just looked at each other and shrugged their shoulders. They both knew it was going to take time for their mother to get used to a new and very different way of life from the one she had known on the river with Thomas.

"Beth, here's the key to the front door," Kenneth said as he put it in her tiny hand. "You help Mama in the house and then we'll get busy," he added as he ran around to the back of the truck and let the tailgate down. "We need to get this unloaded before the rain gets here and it gets any colder. Who knows," he shrugged with a grin, "it may even snow!"

"I sure hope not," Beth replied as she ran around to the other side of the truck and opened the door for her mother. "Let's go inside now, Mama, before you get a chill," she said as she helped Marie out of the truck and, taking her arm, lead her up the few steps to the front porch. As she turned the key in the door, she looked at her mother with excitement. "I know you're gonna love it here, Mama. I just know it!"

Beth let Marie go in first and then she followed. The staircase was right in front of the door, leaving very little room to stand. To the left was the living room and straight through and behind it was the kitchen. Beth saw a tiny switch on the wall by the door and she flipped it up with her finger. When the ceiling light came on, she laughed and jumped up and down and around with sheer joy. No more sitting at the kitchen table trying to do homework by the light of that old oil lamp. She hoped her mother had thrown it away.

"Come in here, squirt," Kenneth called from the kitchen, surprising Beth. He had let himself in the backdoor with the extra key.

Beth darted through the living room and Marie followed slowly. Kenneth was standing in front of a large cabinet with a window over it and water was running out of the faucet and into the sink.

"Mama, Mama, look at this!" Beth exclaimed and immediately went over and began turning the knobs back and forth, making the water stop and start. She could hardly contain her happiness and excitement. "Hot and cold running water! We won't have to heat water on the stove anymore. Won't that be just wonderful, Mama?" Beth asked.

"Yes, Beth," her mother replied. "It's all very nice."

"I want to show you this, Mama," Kenneth said as he opened the back door. "We have a nice backyard where you can sit in the swing under the tree during the summer and do your needlework," he rambled. "And look over here," he said, walking over to the electric stove. "No more cutting wood! All you have to do is turn a knob and these eyes on the stove automatically get hot."

"It's a wonderful thing, all right," she replied with very little enthusiasm, "but don't you think it's time to get the truck unloaded before it starts pouring down rain?" she asked. "Then we can get the beds set up so we'll at least have somewhere to sleep tonight."

It wasn't Marie's intention to take the excitement away from Kenneth and Beth but she had always looked on the practical side. She was glad that they were so excited and she wished that she could share their joy, but there was no joy in her life without Thomas and now there would be no Christmas either.

There was no money for presents this year, but she would try to make the best of it, for the sake of her children. There was no way around it. Life was going to be difficult for her wherever she lived.

Two of the neighbors saw Beth and Kenneth unloading the truck and offered to help them. Kenneth gladly accepted and soon everything was inside and the beds were set up. Then the rain began, just as Kenneth had predicted.

Beth didn't care that it was raining. She didn't even care if it snowed. She just knew she was going to love living here and she snuggled down in her warm, cozy featherbed on this cold winter night. The sound of the rain on the tin roof made drifting off to dreamland extremely easy.

Chapter Five

Sunday morning arrived much too soon for Beth and the rain was still coming down. However, the rain wasn't what made this Sunday morning different from all the other Sunday mornings in Beth's life. This was the first Sunday that she and her family would not go to church. She thought of the many times she had tried to get out of going to church, and now it seemed so strange to her that they actually weren't going. Marie was very sad that they couldn't afford to drive back to the river for church but she was hopeful about finding another church soon that was close by. So, they made the best of the situation and spent this rainy Sunday unpacking and putting away their belongings.

Two bedrooms and a bathroom were located upstairs. Kenneth took the smaller of the two at the end of the hallway at the back of the house and Marie and Beth shared the larger one, which faced the street, with two windows looking out over the front porch.

The bathroom, which also fascinated Beth, was situated between the two bedrooms in the middle of the hallway. Blue, plastic tiles, about four inches square, covered the walls about half way up from the floor. The remaining walls were painted white. A small sink was attached to the wall with a mirror above it that opened. There were shelves inside. Kenneth said it was called a "medicine cabinet" but Beth guessed you could put other things in there, too. The bathtub amazed Beth. It was deep and long and sat up off the floor on four feet. She could hardly wait to take a nice, hot bath in it before going to bed.

Later that night before going to bed, Kenneth explained the public transportation system to Marie and Beth. "The bus stop is on the corner, Mama," he began. "One comes by every thirty minutes and goes downtown. It costs ten cents each way and it runs every day except Sunday. You can go anywhere you want to while I'm at work."

"Thanks, Kenneth," Marie said. "That's good to know. Now, we'd better get to bed. It's been a long day for all of us, and you have to get up early in the morning," she added. As she patted him on the back, they all went upstairs, hoping for a good night's sleep.

Despite a beautiful bright sun, a cold, bitter wind greeted Kenneth when he left for work very early Monday morning. The early hour didn't really bother him that much. He was used to getting up early on the farm and he was excited about starting his new job. His job was one which allowed him to sit down most of the time, which pleased him because his injured leg made it extremely difficult for him to stand up or walk for long periods of time.

Marie decided that since it was so close to Christmas vacation she would wait until the start of the second semester to enroll Beth in school. This pleased Beth immensely. She had always been shy around strangers was extremely nervous about starting to a new school and making new friends. Kenneth had tried to reassure her by telling her that most of the kids that went to this school were children of mill workers, too, and most of them also lived in mill town. Knowing that eased her mind somewhat so she was hopeful that it wouldn't be too hard for her to make new friends after all.

So, given that Kenneth was at work and Beth didn't have to go to school, Marie decided that the two of them would bundle up and take the bus to town. They could spend the entire day just window shopping and exploring. Marie had been to town with Thomas on a few occasions over the years but they had only taken Beth a couple of times when she was very small. Thomas felt that it would only expose her to the worldly things that he knew she would want and he couldn't afford to give her. Marie knew deep down that he was really protecting himself from the hurt of having to say "no" to Beth. However, that was all in the past now and so it was time for both of them to learn that living in the city would be quite different from what their life had been like on the river.

The bus stop was only a few blocks from Beth's house and one came by every half hour. Because of the cold, they left just a few minutes before time for the bus so their wait wouldn't be very long. As they stepped up into the bus, Marie deposited their dimes, one for each of them, in the meter. It was fairly early so there were still plenty of vacant seats in the front of the bus. Beth followed her mother to one close to the driver and they sat down.

Beth looked around the bus at all the people and wondered who they were and where they might be going. It would be her first ride on a bus and she could hardly contain her excitement. However, from the disinterested looks on the faces of the other people, there must not be much excitement about riding a bus. There was one other oddity Beth noticed that aroused her curiosity. "Mama," she said distracting Marie from her own sightseeing out the window, "why are all the colored people sitting in the back of the bus and all the white people in the front?" she questioned curiously.

"That's just the way it is, honey," Marie answered. "Now keep your voice down," she added in a whisper. "We don't want the other people to hear you talking."

Now Beth really was perplexed and confused. "What do you mean, Mama? Can't people talk on the bus either?" she asked.

Boy, Beth thought, *this city life really is going to take some getting used to.*

"Yes, of course you can talk on the bus, but just not too loud," Marie whispered once again. "It's just that some things you don't talk about in public places. You see, Beth, colored people and white people just don't mingle with one another." Marie wasn't very educated on the ways of the city either but she wasn't completely unaware of how things were. "I'll get Kenneth to explain it all to you better later," she promised. "In the meantime, just look out the window and enjoy the sights. We have a few miles to go before we get downtown."

"Yes, Mama," Beth replied.

Content with her mother's answer for now, Beth stretched her neck, trying to look out the window at all the different buildings, cars going by and people milling about the streets. It was all so overwhelming and hard for her to grasp. To her it was like being in another world, a world she suddenly realized was going to be a lot harder to live in than she had first thought. The bus turned down one street after another making many stops to pick up more people, each depositing their dime in the meter slot and taking a seat. Some would also exit the bus at each stop through a side door near the rear. She noticed, too, that no matter how many empty seats there were in the front of the bus, the colored people crowded into the back. This was very confusing. She had been raised around colored people on the river and they had worked side by side in the cotton fields. Big Mose had help save Kenneth's life and he and his wife, Sara and their children had been very close friends of the Benson family. Beth had never given the color difference much thought, until today.

"This is where we get off," Marie said as she shook Beth by the shoulder and brought her out of her thoughts.

Beth was amazed at all the stores and in the center of town was this grand and beautiful building. "What is that building, Mama?" Beth asked pointing in its direction. It seemed to say "I'm important" and demanded everyone's attention.

"That's the county courthouse, honey," Marie answered. "That's where all of the county business is taken care of."

"Oh," Beth acknowledged without much enthusiasm. What she really wanted to do was explore the stores. "Mama, can we please go in one of the stores now?" she asked anxiously.

"Sure," Marie replied smiling at Beth's innocence and excitement.

The first store they went in was JC Penney. Inside were so many beautiful clothes and shoes that Beth thought she was in a fairytale come true. She had never seen such beautiful things and she wanted to touch each and every dress and feel the wonderful material. She had never had a store bought dress and she wanted one now in the worst way.

By now, Beth's excitement made her oblivious to the cold. Their next visit to Montgomery Ward, another department store on the courthouse square, was where Beth saw the most amazing thing of all, a television set. It was almost magical. She hoped with all her heart that they would be able to have one someday. Yes, Beth's first excursion to town was becoming a most memorable one and she looked forward to many more in the near future.

The "colored/white" issue also became more and more evident as Beth and her mother continued to window shop. While in one of the stores by the name of Woolworth's (sometimes called the "five" and "dime,") Beth was thirsty and wanted a drink of water. The clerk told her that the water fountains and restrooms were located in the back of the store. When she reached the fountain, she was surprised to find that there were two, each one mounted to the wall and each one with a sign over it. One had the word "**White**" painted on it and the other one had "**Colored**." The restrooms were marked in the same manner on each door. Two for women and two for men. She would certainly be glad when Kenneth explained these strange "city" ways to her.

Later that evening after supper, Kenneth tried to explain to Beth that colored people and white people lived separate lives in the city. It was called segregation. The colored people couldn't even eat in the same restaurant with white people and they actually had their very own part of town with a movie theatre, stores and restaurants. As a rule, white people didn't venture into the colored part of town. However, a lot of colored people worked for white people. The women were either maids or nannies and the men worked in the yards and gardens and performed other maintenance type work.

Kenneth began to explain. "Many colored people, or as they prefer to be called, blacks, are forming organizations to fight, nonviolently, for their civil rights. One man, in particular, has become very well known for his involvement in the Montgomery Bus Boycott. His name is Dr. Martin Luther King, Jr. He was president of the Montgomery Improvement Association at the time and this was the organization that directed the boycott."

Beth was glued to every word Kenneth was saying. She wondered how he knew so much and could hardly wait to hear more. "What is a bus boycott?" she asked.

"It happened last December, 1955, during my senior year in high school. It all began when Rosa Parks, who was the secretary of the Montgomery Chapter of the NAACP, refused to give up her seat on a Montgomery bus to a white person. She was arrested, tried and convicted on disorderly conduct and for violating a local ordinance. After her arrest, a large group of blacks decided to organize a bus boycott," Kenneth explained.

"Well, you still haven't told me what a bus boycott is," Beth protested with a huff, "and what is the NAACP?" she asked.

"A boycott is when a group of people get together and decide not to do something, like shop at a certain store or to not buy a certain brand product. It's kinda like a protest against something. The NAACP stands for the National Association for the Advancement of Colored People," Kenneth explained. "Now during this particular boycott in Montgomery, all the colored people agreed not to ride the city buses until the city agreed to let them ride the buses with the white people, colored people from the back to the front of the bus and white people from the front to the back. This boycott lasted for over a year and because most of Montgomery's black population participated in the boycott, it worked. The boycott ended last month when a federal court ordered Montgomery's buses desegregated. Does that help you to understand any better, Beth?" Kenneth asked as he smiled and rubbed the top of her head with his hand, mussing her hair on purpose, as usual.

"Not really," Beth answered as she shook her head, in response to both his question and the head rub. She wondered if she would ever understand. It all seemed so unfair to her. Why couldn't people just live together and be happy, regardless of their color? She wasn't sure she agreed with this "city life" at all and decided she was going to have to find out more about this subject. She was still very young and didn't realize it at the time, but she had just been introduced to the civil rights movement which would eventually give birth to integration.

"Kenneth, how did you get to be so smart anyway?" she asked jokingly.

"We studied about this in high school and I read a lot, squirt," he replied. "Racial tensions are growing in the South now, especially after the success of the boycott. Many white people are very much against integration and use violence as a way of getting what they want instead of talking. Some of them even bombed Dr. King's home back in January and personally, I think the violence is just beginning, Beth," he added with a seriousness in his voice that Beth had never heard before. "I want you to be very aware of your surroundings from now on because I'm afraid the situation is only going to get worse," he added with concern. "It's a very different world we live in now and things are changing fast."

Christmas was different this year, too, but not because there was no money for gifts. Celebrating the birth of Jesus was always the focus of Christmas in the Benson house and Thomas always read from the Bible on Christmas Eve. Beth loved to hear him read the story of Mary and Joseph and how baby Jesus was born in the stable. Marie always made hot chocolate and homemade cookies for them to eat while they listened. However, this year, Kenneth took Thomas's place reading the scriptures and even though she still missed her father tremendously, she was thankful that Kenneth was still with them.

Marie managed, as every mother does, to have a gift for Beth and Kenneth under the tree on Christmas morning. She crocheted each of them a set of matching toboggans and gloves to wear on cold, winter days ahead. Yes, love still flourished in the Benson house.

Chapter Six

Her first day of school at Brookhaven Elementary School in January of 1957, came as no surprise to Beth. The classroom was not unlike the one at her old school. Large windows covered the outside wall and were closed now because of the cold but would definitely be raised come spring. The teacher's desk was at one end of the room in front of the large blackboard, which covered most of that wall. As if waiting patiently for class to begin, the chalk and erasers were neatly placed at equal intervals along the metal tray connected to the bottom. Beth smiled as she remembered the many times she had taken the erasers outside and clapped them together to remove the chalk so they would be clean for the next day.

The extremely loud ringing of the bell startled Beth back to reality, and the rows of desks were soon filled with students. She had barely sat down when her greatest fear became a reality. Butterflies consumed her stomach when the teacher asked her to stand up and introduce herself to the entire class. Beth did not like to be the center of attention but since her teacher, a tall, slender middle-aged woman, seemed so very nice, she didn't want to appear uncooperative. As she stood, her eyes began to look over the class and she saw some familiar faces from the village. This made her feel a little less intimidated as she began her mini-autobiography and she was convinced that she would soon have many new friends.

Beth's grades had been transferred from her old school and she knew immediately, from that very first day of class, that she was in deep trouble. The fifth-grade at her old school at the river was far behind this one and she would have to do some serious studying in order to catch up before the end of the school year in May. She certainly didn't want to repeat the fifth grade. So, with Kenneth's help and a lot a determination, May finally arrived and she was promoted, with honors, to the sixth grade.

Beth was all smiles as she entered the kitchen that afternoon carrying her final report card for the year.

"Look, Mama," she exclaimed as she held it out for Marie to see. "I got ALL A's and passed to the sixth grade!"

"That's wonderful, honey," Marie replied as she took the report card from Beth and carefully looked it over. "I'm so proud of you, sweetie!" she added as she gave Beth a big hug. "I never doubted for one minute that you could do it and to celebrate, I'm fixin' your favorite for supper tonight."

"Oh, boy, meatloaf!" Beth screamed with delight. "Are we having pintos and cornbread, too?" she asked with eyes as big as jawbreakers.

"Well now, meatloaf just wouldn't be the same without them, would it?" Marie answered with a laugh as she turned her attention back to the meal preparation at the sink. "Why don't you go outside in the backyard and play until Kenneth gets home. Supper will be ready then."

"OK, Mama," Beth replied and ran out the screened door, letting it slam shut as usual.

Marie was glad to see Beth so happy. The last five months had been difficult for the entire family. Beth adjusting to a new school and new friends and

Kenneth to a new job and routine. Racial tensions had not eased across the state and violence continued. Soon after Beth started to school, the home of Ralph Abernathy, pastor of the First Baptist Church in Montgomery was bombed. He was a close friend of Dr. King. The situation worried Marie but there was nothing she could do. Their life went on one day at a time, just like everyone else they knew.

As they gathered at the table for supper later that evening, Beth was beside herself with excitement as she wondered how she was going to spend her first summer in the city. After buttering a piece of cornbread, she sprinkled it with sugar and set it aside for later. Having that ritual completed, she then began piling her plate high with crumbled cornbread that she covered with pinto beans and bean soup. Some meatloaf and mashed potatoes finished off quite a supper. Little did Beth know, as she sat enjoying her favorite supper on this wonderful last day of school, that her mother had already made plans for her first summer in the city.

"Kenneth, there's something I'd like to talk to you about," Marie said after they had finished supper and she was clearing the table, putting the dirty dishes in the sink to wash.

"Sure, Mama," Kenneth replied wiping his mouth with a napkin. Curious about what his mother wanted to talk to him about, he asked "What's on your mind?"

"I've been doing a lot of thinking about how I could help out with the bills this summer and before you say "NO," I want you to hear me out," she said sternly as she sat back down at the table next to him.

Kenneth and Beth, who was eating her piece of buttered and sugared cornbread, looked at each other with confused looks, wondering what their mother could possibly be wanting to talk to him about.

"O.K., Mama, you have my undivided attention," he declared.

A little less interested in the upcoming conversation, Beth got up and poured some more sweet tea in her glass of ice before sitting back down at the table. Still unable to keep focused on the present, her mind wondered, instead, to the upcoming summer vacation.

"Do you remember Joan Daniels?" Marie asked. "She lives two houses down on the corner."

"Yes, I do," Kenneth answered. "Her son, James, works with me."

"Well," Marie continued, "she got word from a friend of hers that the mayor's wife is looking for someone to make new drapes for her living and dining rooms, so I thought I would call her and see if she's found anyone yet," Marie explained. "Now that school is out for the summer, I can take Beth with me and do the sewing there."

Marie definitely got Beth's attention with that last sentence. At first, she was excited at what her mother was saying. Just the thought of actually getting to go inside the mayor's house and see all their beautiful things was enough to make anyone excited. But on second thought, once she had seen everything, what then?

"Oh, Mama," Beth complained with a sigh. "Just what am I going to do all day while you're sewing?"

"I'll tell you exactly what you'll be doing all day, young lady," Marie intervened without hesitation. "You'll be helping me! Besides, it's time you learned how to sew. It'll come in handy someday when you're older and then you'll thank me for teaching you."

A frown quickly covered Beth's face as she glared up at Kenneth who was standing at the sink pouring himself another glass of tea. She had her doubts that learning to sew would be very much fun and that definitely wasn't how she had wanted to spend her first summer in the city. Taking the bus to town and going to the movies and the swimming pool with friends was more like what she had in mind. One thing was for certain, though. Beth knew when to be quiet, so she just continued to eat her cornbread and listen. Any other action would not result in a good outcome, at least not at this time.

"Well, Mama, it sounds like a wonderful opportunity, if that's what you really want to do," Kenneth agreed wholeheartedly while giving Beth a displeasing look. "You'll get to meet the mayor and his family and it might even lead to some more jobs."

Beth knew that look, too, so once again she just sat quietly.

"It's what I want to do, Kenneth, and getting more work is exactly what I'm counting on," Marie added excitedly. "Surely if she's pleased with my work, she'll tell her friends. I want to help you with the bills."

A little concerned about the enormity of the job though, Kenneth had to ask, "Mama, are you sure it's not too much for you to take on by yourself?"

"No, I don't think so. I'm sure with Beth's help, we'll be able to manage just fine," Marie assured anxiously waiting for Kenneth's reply.

"Well, I guess you should walk down to Mrs. Daniel's and use her telephone to give the mayor's wife a call," Kenneth exclaimed. "Maybe she hasn't found anyone yet. While you're gone, Beth and I will get started washing these dishes," he added as he gave her a big hug. "If you do get this job, we'll all have to pitch in around here from now on for sure."

Marie was anxious to find out, too, and immediately got up from the table. She gave Beth a quick hug and said, "I'll be right back after I talk to her. Keep your fingers crossed," she said as she quickly hurried out the front door.

Beth was not a happy camper and made no attempt to hide it from Kenneth. She looked like she had just lost her best friend, again, but he couldn't let her disappointment influence the situation. This was family survival and "feelings" couldn't get in the way. They could definitely use the extra money, for sure. Beth would just have to suck it up and step up to the plate again, just like before, and do her part. He wished things were different, but life was what it was and working was the only way to make it better. He promised himself, though, that he would also make sure that Beth had some fun times, too, before school started back in the fall. After all, she would only be eleven years old come her birthday in July.

"Let's have these dishes all washed and put away before Mama gets home, squirt," Kenneth said. "Do you want to wash or dry?"

Beth slowly got up from the table and walked over to the sink. "I think I'll wash," she stated as she turned on the faucet and put in the stopper. "Will you raise the window, please? It sure is hot in here tonight," she complained as she added the dishwashing liquid.

"I know this doesn't make you very happy, Beth," Kenneth said as he began to dry the dishes Beth had rinsed and put in the drain rack, "but I think it will be good for both you and Mama. You'll get to meet some new people, Mama will get out of the house and you'll be learning to sew all at the same time."

"Yea, it sounds really great! I can hardly wait!" Beth said sarcastically. "I'll soon be eleven years old and I'm going to have to spend my whole first summer in the city working. How exciting is that?" she asked as she used her arm to move sweat drenched hair from her forehead.

"Now, squirt," Kenneth implored. "It won't be all that bad and I promise to take you to the movies and you're old enough to ride the bus with some of your friends to the pool downtown. We might even be able to go see Roslyn and Richard a few times, too. That is, if that old truck holds together," he added with a laugh.

His last statement put that familiar smile that Kenneth loved to see back on Beth's face. "Thanks, I'd like that very much," Beth said feeling a little ashamed of herself. "I'm sorry I acted that way. I really do hope that Mama gets this job."

"Me, too," Kenneth answered and just as the last dish was dried and put away, they heard Marie as she came through the front door.

"I talked to Mrs. Cole on the telephone and she hasn't found anyone yet," Marie stated excitedly as she entered the kitchen. "She wants me to come to her house Monday morning at ten o'clock so she can show me what she wants. She said if I still wanted the job after that, we would discuss the pay," she added breathlessly. "So, what do you think?"

"I think it's been a great day for the Benson family," Kenneth replied with enthusiasm as he and Beth hugged their mother close.

The weekend passed uneventfully and a Monday morning sun burst forth on the horizon. Yes, thought Marie, it is going to be a beautiful, sunny day. However, she found herself more than a little nervous about meeting the mayor's wife. So much so that she decided to take the nine o'clock bus to ensure that they wouldn't be late.

The mayor's house was located downtown in the historical district, just a few blocks from the courthouse square. The bus ride seemed to take forever as Beth became increasingly fidgety in her seat. The dress her mother had picked out for her to wear didn't help the situation either. The petticoat kept scratching her on the back of her legs. Finally, and much to her delight, the bus reached its destination downtown. It was only a three-block walk to the mayor's house and Beth's excitement grew with each step.

"How much further is it, Mama?" Beth asked impatiently. It seemed as though they had walked for miles.

"We're here," Marie answered without hesitation.

Beth could hardly believe her eyes when she saw the grandness of the house as she and her mother walked through the ornate, iron gate. A very wide and long, concrete sidewalk lined with tiny white flowers on both sides led to the huge wrap-around front porch, which was adorned with hanging ferns. A white wicker basket full of pink and white impatiens claimed a spot on each side of the front door. It was the biggest door Beth had ever seen, with a large oval glass with a colored stained-glass design in the center. There was a long, narrow window on each side of the huge door and a big half-circle window over the top of the door. She looked around at the yard full of workers who were busy planting spring flowers in the many flowerbeds around the beautiful, tree-filled green yard. It sure was beautiful, she thought. Marie's hand shook as she reached out to push the brass doorbell. She and Beth anxiously waited for the door to open.

Their wait wasn't long. Almost immediately, the front door opened and a black lady, dressed in a pale gray dress with a white collar and a starched white apron, politely greeted Marie and Beth with a smile.

"Hello, you must be Mrs. Benson," she said politely.

"Yes, I am," replied Marie with a smile, "and this is my daughter, Beth," she added as she gestured toward Beth.

"Please, come in," the lady replied motioning for Marie and Beth to enter. "If you'll follow me to the living room, Mrs. Cole is expecting you."

"Thank you," Marie said as she and Beth followed her into the living room, which was to the left of the large, beautiful foyer.

Beth couldn't believe the beauty that her eyes engulfed. The grand magnificence of the room took her breath away.

"Mrs. Cole, Mrs. Benson is here," said the lady in the gray dress.

"Thank you, Mae. You may go now," Mrs. Cole said to the woman as she smiled and held out her hand to Marie.

Beth was awestruck and couldn't take her eyes off Mrs. Cole. She was a strikingly beautiful woman with red hair and emerald green eyes. Her teeth were perfect and as white as new-fallen snow. Beth felt as though she had been magically transported into a fairy tale and she was, at the very least, a princess.

"It's so nice to meet you, Mrs. Benson," she said in a sweet voice.

"Likewise," Marie answered and even though she felt somewhat intimidated in her handmade, flour sack dress, she shook Marilyn Cole's outstretched hand with confidence and returned her warm smile. "This is my daughter, Beth," Marie added looking at Beth.

"Please, call me Marilyn. I'm not much on formality when I'm not at some political function for my husband. It makes me so uncomfortable," Marilyn said as she looked down at Beth with a smile that could melt butter. *What a beautiful child,* she thought. No prettier one had she ever seen.

"Hello, Beth," she said as she put her hand softly on Beth's shoulder. "It's my pleasure to meet you. You are a beautiful little girl," she added making Beth feel very welcome and comfortable in these extravagant surroundings.

"Thank you, Mrs. Cole," Beth replied. "It's nice to meet you, too."

"Is Beth short for Elizabeth?" she asked.

"Yes, ma'am," Beth answered. "My whole name is Rachel Elizabeth Benson. The Rachel part is after my grandmother," she decided to add.

"That's a very beautiful name, Beth," she said. "As a matter of fact, my daughter's name is also Elizabeth. Margaret Elizabeth, to be exact, after each of her grandmothers. She is finishing her sophomore year at Auburn University in a couple of weeks but has decided to stay and take a couple of classes this summer. We will surely miss her around here."

Looking back at Marie, Marilyn asked, "May I offer you some coffee or other beverage?"

"No, but thank you anyway," Marie politely declined fighting her compulsion to admire the beautiful room that surrounded them instead of her hostess.

Beth had quietly watched earlier when Mae left the room. Never having seen one before, she couldn't help but wonder if she might be the maid. Most rich people had one and surely the mayor had to be rich. His wife sure did look rich and they had this beautiful house and all these beautiful things. Beth wanted to be rich someday. She just didn't know right now how that was going to happen. Time was on her side though, so she didn't have to worry about that right now.

"Please, Mrs. Benson, let's sit on the sofa," Marilyn said as she walked toward the large sofa covered in a red and gold tapestry fabric. "Tell me a little bit about yourself and your family then I'll tell you what I need."

As the two women proceeded to sit down on the sofa, Marilyn glanced back at Beth. She just couldn't get over how beautiful she was.

"Beth, you may sit by your mother if you'd like," Marilyn said.

"Thank, you, ma'am and I hope to go to college someday, too," Beth added much to her own surprise and worried that she had spoken out of turn.

"That's a wonderful ambition for someone so young. I hope all your dreams come true, my dear. How old are you?" she asked.

"I'll be eleven in July," Beth replied proudly.

"Well, you have plenty of time to make that dream come true," Marilyn added with a smile. "I have certainly enjoyed meeting you, Beth, but now, your mother and I have some business to discuss. So, if you don't mind, there's a very nice swing in the backyard if you'd like to pass the time there. If you get hot or thirsty, just tell Mae and she will be glad to get you something cool to drink."

"Thank you, Mrs. Cole," Beth said as she rose from the sofa then quickly left the room, hurrying out the front door. Alone on the porch, she took a deep, cleansing breath and relaxed for the first time since entering the house. Once again her eyes marveled at the beauty of the yard as she slowly walked down the steps and followed the sidewalk around to the back of the house. Most of the trees, such as Bradford Pear, Red Bud, and Dogwoods had already bloomed. The azaleas, too, had already finished their spring display but Beth could tell by all the many flats of flowers, such as impatiens and begonias still to be planted, that the yard would be beautiful this summer. It was while on this expedition of the yard that Beth found the wicker swing Mrs. Cole had told her about. *The mayor's wife sure does like wicker,* Beth thought. *I might just have me some wicker furniture someday.* After taking a seat in the swing, a black girl, about her age, caught Beth's eye. She was standing over by the pool house. Beth's curiosity grew as she watched the girl hand flowers to the man who was then planting them in a flower bed surrounded by a border of dark green mondo grass. As she continued to watch the two plant flowers, Mae came out of the back door with what looked like a glass of lemonade in one hand and a pitcher in the other. She walked over to the girl and said something to her. They were too far away for Beth to hear what they were saying, but that didn't keep her from being curious. Mae didn't give the little girl the lemonade but instead started walking toward Beth.

"This is for you, Miss Beth," she said with a smile as she handed the glass to Beth. "It'll be gettin' mighty hot out here b'fore long and you could be out here quite some time 'cause Mrs. Cole sure do love to talk."

Beth was a little bewildered and wondered why she was the only one getting lemonade. "Thank you," she said politely as she took the glass offered to her and took a sip of the ice cold lemonade. She was thirstier than she thought and drank the entire glass without stopping. It was the best lemonade she had ever tasted. "That was really good!" she exclaimed as she tried to discretely wipe her mouth.

Having gulped down the lemonade, and Beth being Beth, she thought nothing of asking about the girl by the pool house. "Who is that girl over there?" she asked pointing in the direction where the girl was standing.

"Oh, she's my daughter, Eliza Jane," Mae answered. "She'll be eleven years old on July 19th. That's her daddy she's helpin'. I 'spect she'll be here a lot this summer."

"Well, what about that!" Beth exclaimed jubilantly. "That's exactly when my birthday is, too, and we're the same age! I guess I'll be here a lot this summer, too," Beth added. "That is if my mother gets the job making Mrs. Cole's new drapes. Maybe Eliza Jane and I can play together and be friends."

"Oh no, Miss Beth, that wouldn't be proper," Mae said sadly.

Here was this black/white thing coming up again, Beth thought. Why was life so unfair? They were just two little girls and she didn't see a problem at all with them becoming friends and didn't hesitate to tell Mae exactly how she felt. That was Beth being Beth again.

"I don't see anything wrong with it myself," Beth began justifying her position on the subject as she did on a lot of other subjects. "Both of our mothers would be working for Mrs. Cole. Both of us are going to be here helping our mothers so that would make us all "workers" and that would make us all alike."

"It sounds very simple the way you put it, Miss Beth, but that just ain't the way things is, chile," Mae remarked, "Best you just not think about you and

Eliza Jane being friends," she added as she poured Beth some more lemonade. "You needs to just get that outta yo' mind right here and now," she added in no uncertain terms.

Before Beth could make another comment on the subject, Mae turned and slowly walked down the sidewalk, then disappeared into the house.

Beth contemplated what Mae had just said as she continued to swing. She took a long drink of her second glass of lemonade, all the while looking at Eliza Jane. She looked to be about Beth's size but maybe a little taller. Her black hair was in two braids that were pinned on top of her head. Her dress looked just like Beth's flour sack dress except it had pink flowers on it and Beth's were yellow. So, what was so different? Just the color of their skin and hair was all. She looked like a nice person, Beth thought, as she continued to watch her hand the flowers to her father. *I'm sure we'll become really good friends,* Beth decided, and when Beth made up her mind to something, she usually found a way to make it happen. Now all she had to do was figure out how.

"Beth, honey, where are you?" came Marie's voice from out of nowhere. Startled, Beth jumped from the swing. Not knowing what to do with her glass, she just sat it on the ground then ran to meet her mother, who was standing on the sidewalk at the side of the house.

"I got the job!" Marie exclaimed with joy as she gave Beth a hug.

"I'm so glad, Mama, and Kenneth will be, too," Beth replied happily.

Arm and arm, mother and daughter walked toward the bus stop both happy and both wondering what the next day of their life would bring.

Chapter Seven

The next several years passed quickly and by the summer of 1960, Beth had learned the ways of the city. Some she liked and some she didn't. The part she disliked the most was how some people, both blacks and whites, felt about her and Eliza Jane's friendship. They had become very close friends since their first meeting at the mayor's house in the summer of 1957, despite the growing racial unrest in the South.

Marie had continued to work for Mrs. Cole which made it easy for Beth and Eliza Jane to see each other during the summers. Then, in the fall, Mayor Cole lost his bid for re-election and as a result, Marie lost her job. Sadly, Beth would not get to see very much of Eliza Jane that coming summer. However, throughout all the turmoil, they continued their friendship by writing letters when they weren't able to see or talk to one another.

Summer came, and with it Beth got exciting news. She, Roslyn, and Richard were no longer going to be apart. Sadly, Bill Hartman had suffered a heart attack earlier in the year making it impossible for him to continue working on the farm. With Kenneth's help, he was able to get a job at the mill as a security guard and the Hartmans had moved to mill town as soon as school was out, bringing the threesome back together once again.

On the political front, a very handsome young senator from Massachusetts by the name of John F. Kennedy was running for President of the United States. Beth and Roslyn both thought he was extremely handsome, as did all of the teenage girls.

On July 15, the fourth anniversary of her father's death, John Kennedy won the democratic nomination and Beth celebrated her fourteenth birthday four days later. The real celebration ensued in the Benson house when he was elected president that November.

John Kennedy was sworn in as the nation's 35th President on January 20, 1961, and the following months were filled with life changing events. In April, the Russians launched the first man into outer space and in May, Alan Shepard became the first American in outer space. Beth was extremely excited about current events and as her interest in politics grew, so did the civil rights movement in Alabama. By May of that same year, it had reached a new level of intensity. "Freedom Riders," a racially integrated group of activists rode Greyhound and Trailways buses across the state. Needless to say, tensions were extremely high in the south.

"Kenneth, wake up!" Beth whispered, not wanting to wake her mother. "It's Mother's Day and we need to make Mama's breakfast before we go to church," she continued as she shook him by the shoulder.

Kenneth slowly opened his eyes and tried to focus. Rolling over on his back, he stretched his arms up over his head as he looked at Beth. "What did you say, squirt?" he asked sleepily while rubbing his eyes.

"It's Mother's Day and we need to fix Mama's breakfast before we go to church," Beth answered.

"That's a great idea," Kenneth agreed. "You go on and get started and I'll be right there."

"O.K.," Beth answered and was out the door in a flash.

Kenneth, clad only in his white boxer shorts, sat up in his old iron bed and looked around his sparsely furnished, white-walled bedroom. His mind wondered to that summer day Thomas took him to an old flea market in some small town about five miles south of the river. He paid a man five dollars for the iron bed and loaded it in the back of the truck. He couldn't have been more than five or six years old. Later that same summer, Mrs. McDonald was buying new furniture and asked Thomas if they could use a dresser that she was going to give away. Thomas said yes, of course, and there it was sitting against the wall opposite his bed. The walls were bare. With the exception of the blue curtains on the window, which he kept closed to keep out the light, the room was void of color. Maybe he would be able to do something to his room next year.

Knowing that he needed to get up, Kenneth swung his legs over the side of the bed, put his feet on the bare wooden floor and hung his head. His entire body ached from the twelve hours overtime he had worked the day before. All he wanted to do right now was sleep but that would have to wait.

I thought things would be much better by now, Kenneth thought as he walked down the hall to the bathroom. After washing his face, he returned to his bedroom and put on some cut-off blue jean shorts and a tee shirt and joined Beth in the kitchen. Before long they had a wonderful Mother's Day breakfast prepared for Marie.

"Now all we need is some flowers for the table," Beth said, "and I know just where to get them," she added as she ran out the back door.

The next door neighbor had a huge pink azalea bush in the back yard next to the back fence and Beth couldn't resist breaking off a few stems. She put them in a glass of water in the middle of the table, which she had covered with a bright, floral tablecloth, and then ran upstairs to get Marie.

"Oh my goodness!" Marie exclaimed with surprise when she walked into the kitchen. "How sweet of you two to fix my breakfast. Everything looks so good and the flowers are just beautiful! Can't imagine where you got them, Beth," she added with a grin.

"Thank you, Mama," Kenneth and Beth replied in unison.

"We wanted Mother's Day to start off special for you, Mama," Beth added with a smile.

"Well, you have certainly done that and I thank you very much," Marie replied as she pulled a chair out and, fixing her pink, cotton housecoat just right, sat down to enjoy this special breakfast. "Now let's eat before it gets cold or we'll be late for church."

Marie's comment reminded Beth of the years they attended the Calvary Baptist Church when they lived on the river. She liked The First Baptist Church and Rev. Henderson, but it just wasn't the same. It was a larger church and didn't have that close family feel like her old church, and let's not forget the Rev. Jenkins. No one preached like he did. Beth had not had a shiver run down her spine since she last sat in a pew at the Calvary Baptist Church.

Following the services that morning, which honored all the mothers in the congregation, Beth and her family enjoyed a Sunday dinner of leftovers from the night before. Beth was finishing up in the kitchen before settling in for a quiet afternoon at home. That was about all you could do on Sunday in 1961 because all retail businesses were closed.

Marie caught Beth's eye as she entered the living room. She paused quietly in the doorway, not wanting to distract her mother who was sitting on the sofa reading Sunday paper. Beth was very proud of her mother. She had bought the living room furniture with her own money she made while working for Mrs.

Cole. Kenneth had wanted to help but she insisted that she could pay for it herself. The three-cushion sofa and matching chair were upholstered in a gold tweed fabric and the set came with two oak French Provincial end tables and a coffee table. Two lamps completed the set, which Marie told Beth she could pick out when they went to the furniture store. The ones she picked were beautiful and Marie agreed. Made of brass with white shades, the bottom was a white globe, maybe half the size of a basketball. When you pushed the tiny button on the side of the base, a light came on inside the globe. They were the prettiest thing Beth had ever seen and she couldn't believe they were actually sitting in their living room.

A smile came across Beth's lips when she saw Kenneth relaxing in his navy blue and gold plaid recliner. Marie insisted that he buy it with some of his overtime money. He had positioned it at an angle beside the stairway which allowed him to recline and watch television with no problem. A small round table sat beside the chair. The television was an unexpected but very welcomed purchase. A friend of Kenneth's was selling his old one for practically nothing, so now the Bensons had a television, too, something Beth had wanted for a long time.

Kenneth had also enlisted the help of friends and painted the living room in a very light, soft gold and Marie's handmade Brocade drapes were gorgeous on the windows.

Beth was very proud of the man Kenneth had become and she knew their father would have been proud, too. He had worked very hard since moving to the city and had kept his promise to take care of them. She felt very blessed on this Mother's Day.

"I'll be upstairs in my room studying if anyone needs me," Beth said as she walked through the living room to the stairs.

"We'll be right here, squirt," Kenneth replied his eyes never leaving the television.

"Don't strain your eyes," Marie chimed in. "You don't want to have to get glasses."

"I won't, Mama," she promised as she climbed the stairs to her room.

Everything in the bedroom Beth shared with her mother was old. She would be so glad when they could finally afford some new furniture. Beth especially wanted a desk more than anything. She was so tired of having to study while sitting in her feather bed.

"Beth, Beth, come down here quick," echoed Kenneth's scream up the stairwell.

Thinking something must be wrong with her mother, Beth bolted down the stairs with her heart in her throat only to find Kenneth glued to the television.

"What is it, Kenneth?" she asked. "You nearly scared me to death! I thought something was wrong with Mama!" she exclaimed with a huff after seeing that Marie was fine and was watching television, too.

"Sorry, Beth. I didn't mean to scare you but I wanted you to see what's on the news," Kenneth answered as he motioned for her to sit beside him.

Beth couldn't believe what she was hearing. Two hundred white men had attacked the first bus of Freedom Riders with bats and pipes when it arrived in Anniston, Alabama, earlier that afternoon and then firebombed it. Beth was appalled that anyone, whatever color, could do such a horrible thing.

An unexplainable concern came over Beth and she immediately got up and went straight to the telephone. "I need to call Eliza Jane," she said.

Eliza Jane answered.

"Eliza Jane, it's Beth. I was wondering if you had seen the news?" she asked with concern.

"If you're asking about the bus attack, yes I have," Eliza Jane replied. "I'm so scared, Beth. It makes me afraid of what's going to happen next."

"I know. It does me, too," Beth answered.

"I called to tell you how sorry I am about what happened and that not all white people are like the ones who did that terrible thing," Beth tried to explain.

"Beth, I'm really trying to believe that right now but it's hard, you know?" Eliza Jane replied.

"I know. I wish things were different, too, and this whole situation could somehow be handled without all the violence," Beth responded trying to be positive.

"Thank you for calling, Beth. I know you are a good friend and are not like these hateful, mean people."

"I'm glad you feel that way. I'll talk to you soon, Eliza Jane," Beth added before hanging up the phone.

"What did she say, squirt?" asked Kenneth when Beth sat back down beside him.

"She's sad and very disheartened," Beth answered sadly.

Chapter Eight

Summer came and along with it, the "oh so familiar" heat, but life went on as usual in the Benson house. Kenneth was still working at the mill and Beth helped her mother with sewing jobs she managed to get occasionally. The anticipation of being a sophomore in high school in the fall began to consume Beth's thoughts. This proved to be somewhat unnerving the closer it got to September. Students from several other junior high schools would also be attending the same high school, students whose families were more affluent than hers and didn't work at the mill. The only thing that made her a little less anxious was the fact that Roslyn and Richard would be there, too.

After the start of school that fall of 1961, Beth quickly learned that prejudice and discrimination didn't just exist between whites and blacks. It existed between the "haves" and the "have nots." This was a situation Beth had not been privy to until now. Students from the "mill town" were shunned by most of the students from the more affluent neighborhoods and Beth was no exception. She suffered daily humiliation from their prejudice, ridicule and sometimes, even cruelty. Many of the girls were jealous of Beth's beauty and ignored her completely. Eventually, Beth gave up trying to make friends and made venturing beyond her own friends against her rules. The situation did, however, help Beth to better understand what the black people fighting for their civil rights were feeling. For in her own world among white people, she was also being segregated and ostracized, not because of her color, but because of her family's financial status.

Instead of letting this situation defeat her though, it made her stronger and more determined than ever to make a successful life for herself. Her first priority would be to set a goal and she knew exactly what it would be. She would be her class valedictorian at her graduation, not only to make Kenneth and her mother proud, but to show everyone who had scorned her that she was someone special, regardless of her station in life. So, Beth immersed herself in studying. Any subject to do with Government was her favorite and she followed Kennedy's presidency and current events closely, especially the civil rights movement. Before she realized it, the school year was almost over.

"Beth, where are you?" Roslyn's voice resonated up the staircase from Beth's living room.

"I'm in my room," Beth called back. "Come on up."

Roslyn, her hair in a swinging ponytail, cleared the steps two at a time and bounced into Beth's room where she immediately plopped down on Marie's bed, which was just across from Beth's.

"That was fast!" declared a surprised Beth, who was sitting in the middle of her feather bed, legs folded, with open books spread all around her. "What's up?" she asked a very excited looking Roslyn.

"What's up with you?" asked a perplexed Roslyn. "It's Saturday for goodness sake! What are you doing studying on a Saturday?"

"I study every day, Roz, you know that. I have to if I'm going to be the class valedictorian," Beth answered. "Now, what's going on with you today?"

"Well, for one thing, I need your help. So, you can't study today!" Roslyn declared emphatically.

"What do you mean I can't study today?" asked a confused Beth.

"I've got some news you're not going to believe, so hold onto your hat!" she exclaimed, barely able to contain her excitement. "I got asked to the Junior Prom!" she screamed with jubilation as she bounced up and down on the side of the bed, ponytail swinging.

"You're kidding me," Beth gasped with surprise, putting her hand to her chest. "When did this happen and who asked you?" she demanded to know as she stood up in the middle of the bed with her hands on her hips.

"Well, it happened yesterday during lunch and his name is David Morgan," Roslyn answered with just a hint of hesitation. "And he's a junior, of course, and the quarterback on the football team!"

Beth jumped off the bed and sat down next to Roslyn. "And why am I just now hearing about this David person?" she asked boldly as if she were Roslyn's mother. "I suppose you've already been out with him, too, and didn't even bother tell your very best friend," she scolded.

"Yes, Beth, you're right," Roslyn admitted, "and I should have told you already. I'm sorry but I really wasn't keeping it a secret, though. I just haven't found the right time to tell you. Besides, we've only been out a few times and he's actually a really nice guy. I just know you're going to like him," she added smiling.

Beth's mood suddenly became serious and she stood up and slowly walked over to the raised windows which looked out onto the street below. It was a beautiful, sunny May morning and the warm breeze blew her hair back making the sweat on her face obvious. Her pink shorts and sleeveless blouse was the best she could do to combat the increasing heat. She stared out at all the beautiful trees, already sporting their new summer foliage and thought about what Roslyn had just told her. The prom was the very last event before the school year ended. She was truly happy for Roslyn but couldn't help but feel a little sad for herself, for she had decided there would be no time for dating in her future, and she had to stay true to her convictions. Accomplishing her goal would require a tremendous amount of studying and that was more important than dating. Besides the boys from mill town were rough and not exactly her type. She hoped with all her heart that David wasn't one of them.

Not wanting to spoil her best friend's excitement, Beth turned around and with a broad smile on her face replied with a laugh, "I'm just kidding with you,

Roz. If you like him, I'm positive I will, too," she reassured.

"I can't wait for you to meet him," Roslyn responded excitedly as she stood up and walked over to Beth, "and you know you have to help me find a dress," she added, quickly changing the subject. "We only have two weeks, Beth! That's why you can't study today! Will you please go shopping with me today?" she begged. "Please!"

Beth finally gave in to Roslyn's non-stop pleading. She never could say "no" to Roslyn. "Sure, Roz. We can go this afternoon, after lunch."

"No, No," Roslyn argued. "Let's go right now. It will probably take us all day and we can get some lunch somewhere while we're in town."

Beth had never seen Roslyn so excited. "Well, can I at least change clothes?" Beth asked laughing at her friend's excitement.

"You look great, Beth, but if you absolutely have to then go ahead," Roslyn replied. "I'll meet you at the bus stop in 15 minutes," she added as she flew out the door and down the steps.

It was 10:30 when Beth met Roslyn at the bus stop. The ride to town was uncomfortable, to say the least, and Beth was glad to finally be walking down the sidewalk. She loved everything about downtown but she especially loved the big, old courthouse with its huge four-sided clock on top that chimed on the hour. The green lawn was gorgeous and huge trees encircled the entire building. Park benches lined the sidewalk, giving shoppers a nice place to rest. This was her favorite place in all of downtown.

"Where do you want to start?" Beth asked Roslyn as they continued making their way through the Saturday shoppers crowding the sidewalk.

"Where would you go if you were looking for a prom dress?" Roslyn answered with her own question.

"How much money do you have?" asked Beth, figuring that was the best place to start.

"$20," Roslyn replied softly.

Beth stopped dead in her tracks and, without any thought to the people around them, glared at Roslyn in total disbelief. "Are you serious?" she asked rather loudly with hands on her hips. "You drug me downtown on that hot bus and that's all the money you have! What in the world kind of prom dress can you buy with $20?" she begged to know.

Roslyn felt somewhat disappointed in herself, to say the least. "I'm sorry, Beth," she apologized. "I was so excited about going to the prom, I guess I wasn't thinking about what the dress would cost."

Beth couldn't help but laugh and put a comforting arm around Roslyn's shoulder. "My sweet, sweet Roz. You are my very best friend, even if you are a little naïve sometimes. I guess I'll forgive you this time. After all, neither one of us has ever been to a prom so how do we know what a dress costs. Right? So, let's start with Montgomery Ward," Beth suggested. "I'm sure they will have something that you can afford."

"Fine with me," Roslyn agreed without hesitation.

So, with that decision made, the two headed for the courthouse square. It was only a couple of blocks and the store was on the south side facing the courthouse.

Upon entering the big, double front doors, Beth found a sales associate and asked where they would find the prom dresses. She was told to go down the wide staircase to the downstairs department. This was where all the formal clothes were located.

Once downstairs, Beth and Roslyn stood and just looked at each other with disbelief on their faces. This gigantic room with full-length mirrors on all four walls was breaming over with gorgeous wedding gowns and prom dresses of all sizes, styles and colors. Roslyn couldn't believe her eyes and Beth was simply awestruck. This was a first for them both.

"Well, who would have thought," Roslyn declared as her eyes led her straight towards a red, taffeta dress that had immediately caught her eye. It was covered with layer upon layer of matching chiffon. The fitted bodice had thin shoulder straps and was attached to a full skirt that went all the way to the floor with two rows of ruffles around the bottom. "Isn't this one absolutely beautiful, Beth?" she asked as she held it up next to her and checked the size.

"My size, too!" she squealed as she jumped up and down with joy. "That's a sign! It's meant for me to have this dress! I just know it!" she declared with complete, and unbridled certainty.

"I might have known you'd find a RED one!" Beth teased. "I have to admit, Roz, it's definitely your color and it looks absolutely beautiful against your hair and complexion," she continued with a smile. "How much is it?"

Roslyn's eyes were glued to Beth as she held the price tag in her shaking hand, afraid to look.

"Well?" Beth urged. "You have to look sooner or later, Roz. We can't stay in here all day you know."

Roslyn slowly raised the price tag and forced her eyes to look. "Oh, no," she cried out in horror. "It's $32. That's $12 more than I have. I love this dress, Beth. I just have to have it!!" she declared. "But how?"

"Calm down, Roz," Beth said as she tried to think of a solution. "O.k., here's what we can do. Use your $20 and put the dress on lay-away. That gives us two weeks to come up with the rest of the money."

"And what if we can't get the money?" Roslyn asked with concern.

"Well, then you lose your $20 and you don't have a dress for the prom," Beth answered jokingly.

Roslyn's eyes widened in disbelief at Beth's seemingly unconcerned attitude. "Beth!" she wailed. "How can you joke at a time like this?"

"I'm sorry, Roz," Beth replied with a smile. "You just need to stop worrying so much. We can both make more than that in two weeks just by babysitting and I'll donate mine to the cause," she added. "Now take that dress and go put it on lay-away so we can get some lunch. All this shopping hoopla has made me awfully hungry!"

Even though Roslyn wasn't completely convinced that Beth's plan would work, she didn't have a better one so they hurried upstairs to the lay-away department where she gave them the dress and her $20. Excited, nervous and scared, she tried to appear calm as she and Beth made their way through the store and out the front door.

Yes, life was good, thought Beth, as the two best friends happily made their way through the crowded downtown sidewalks and headed for the Krystal to eat lunch.

With much determination and relentless solicitation from every neighbor in mill town, Beth and Roslyn managed to earn enough money babysitting to retrieve the prom dress from lay-away, and with only two days to spare. Now, as the final hour approached, Roslyn sat in front of the dresser mirror in her bedroom, a complete basket case, while Beth tried to fix her hair.

"You've got to be still, Roz," Beth urged, "or I'll still be here working on this hair of yours when David gets here!"

"Don't scold me, Beth," Roslyn pleaded. "I'm nervous enough as it is."

"Everything's going to be just fine. Just one more pin right here in the back and I'll be through," Beth assured as she put the final pin in exactly the right place. "There, all done and you look absolutely gorgeous!" Beth exclaimed. "You'll be the bell of the ball for sure."

Roslyn hugged Beth tightly. "Thank you so much, Beth," she proclaimed. "If it weren't for your help, I wouldn't even be going to the prom. You are the best friend ever!"

"I know you would do the same for me," Beth replied. "Now you'd better get downstairs. David will be here any minute!"

David couldn't take his eyes off Roslyn when she opened the door to greet him. Beth stood quietly in the background while she introduced him to her parents and Richard. They made a handsome couple, Beth thought, as she watched Bill and David shake hands while Elizabeth pinned on Roslyn's corsage of tiny, white rose buds laying on a bed of greenery and white tulle. Everything was perfect, Beth thought, and as tears began to glisten in her eyes, she silently slipped into the kitchen and out the back door. She could meet David some other time.

The last week of school was busy with final exams and the only thing left for Beth to do now was go to the Board of Education building downtown and get herself a work permit. She wouldn't be sixteen until

July and both she and Roslyn wanted to find a summer job as soon as possible. After considering their options, they decided to start at Woolworth's Five & Dime. It seemed like as good a place as any to begin their search for employment. Decision made, they were to meet at the bus stop at 10:00 a.m. on Monday morning.

The morning sun was already getting hot as Beth and Roslyn made their way to the Board of Education building. Beth was normally a very patient person, but it seemed to take forever to get all the paperwork done for their work permits. However, once they had them in hand, it didn't take long to walk the three blocks to Woolworth's Five & Dime.

"Did everyone decide to come to town today?" Beth asked in exasperation. "Seems to be a lot of people in town for a Monday, but it is almost lunch time. Would you like to eat first, Roz?" she asked as they continued to make their way down the sidewalk.

"Sure, Beth," Roslyn agreed. "I can always eat!"

"That didn't take much urging," Beth laughed. "After we eat we'll find the office and fill out our application. Sure hope we can get a job."

Persistence finally persevered and they made it their destination. Beth opened the door for Roslyn and a rush of cool air welcomed them. Once inside, they made their way to the lunch counter located on the far side of the store.

"Looks like everyone else had the same idea, Beth," answered Roslyn as they looked for a place to sit. "It's so crowded, we might not be able to find a table."

Roslyn had barely gotten the words out of her mouth when Beth suddenly came to an abrupt stop, causing Roslyn to bump into her and nearly knocking her down.

"I'm sorry, Beth," Roslyn apologized. "What's wrong?"

Beth couldn't speak. Her eyes were glued to a booth over by the wall. Were they playing tricks on her or was that really Eliza Jane sitting in that booth? An open Bible lay on the table in front of her.

Slowly, as if in a trance, Beth began to make her way over to the booth and Roslyn followed. It was then that Roslyn realized what was happening. That girl must be Eliza Jane, she thought. She knew about her but they had never met. Whatever Beth was about to do couldn't be a good idea so Roslyn grabbed her by the arm.

"What are you going to do, Beth," Roslyn asked in a low voice.

Once again Beth didn't answer and continued walking toward the booth. In so doing, she had managed to gain the attention of everyone else in the room and the silence was eerie. They all had, of course, simply been ignoring the young black girl sitting alone in an all-white lunch counter and now they wondered what this young white girl was going to do.

"Eliza Jane, what do you think you're doing?" Beth asked in a whisper.

Eliza Jane continued to look straight ahead, avoiding eye contact with Beth. "Beth, you don't understand," she whispered so no one else could hear. "I'm only sitting here as a peaceful protest and you shouldn't be talking to me."

"I do understand, but you are a 15 year-old girl," Beth argued "and you shouldn't be here. You know about all the violence that's been happening. What if someone in here doesn't like your peaceful protest and decides to cause trouble? You could get hurt or even worse!"

"I don't want you to get in trouble, Beth, so just walk away, please. I'll be just fine," Eliza Jane insisted.

Beth couldn't help but worry about Eliza Jane but she also realized that she had to do what she felt she could to help the movement and Beth respected her for that.

"If that's what you want, Eliza Jane, I'll respect your wishes but please stay in touch," Beth stated as she turned and slowly walked away.

"Let's get out of here, Roslyn," Beth said as she walked past her and headed for the door. "I think we can find somewhere else to eat that's not so crowded."

Chapter Nine

Roslyn and Beth both managed to find jobs that summer of '62 and the time passed quickly. School began in September without incident, and the Truman High School football team was having an undefeated season, winning six straight games through October 19th. Since David was the team quarterback, Roslyn insisted that Beth attend every game with her. The entire school was excited about a possible city championship. So, was it any wonder that this was all Roslyn had talked about for six straight weeks. However, this Monday night was all Beth's. She needed a break and had told Roslyn that she would be studying all night.

"That sure was a good supper, Mama. Do you want some help with the dishes?" Beth asked as she took her plate over to the sink and placed it in the hot, soapy dishwater. "Kenneth wants to watch the news so I'll be glad to help you."

"Thank you, Beth, but I can manage," Marie answered. "There's not that many dishes tonight and I know you're tired from school and all. Why don't you go in the living room and visit with Kenneth. I'll be in in a few minutes."

Beth gave Marie a kiss on the cheek and said, "O.K., Mama, I think I will, at least for a little while. Then I'll go on upstairs and do some more studying," she added as she left the kitchen.

Kenneth was sitting on the sofa with his feet up on the coffee table when Beth entered the living room.

"Come sit here by me, squirt," he said as he patted the sofa cushion with his hand. "You've been so busy since school started I haven't seen much of you."

"Are you ever going to stop calling me that?" Beth asked as she sat down.

"Probably, not," Kenneth answered with a laugh.

Before Beth could respond to Kenneth's comment, a news bulletin flashed upon the television screen.

"I wonder what this bulletin is about," Kenneth said as they waited anxiously to hear.

Their wait wasn't long and a news correspondent appeared and said that President Kennedy would be speaking from the White House to the American people in a few minutes.

"Wonder what this could be about," Kenneth said as President Kennedy appeared on the screen.

He announced that a Soviet missile site capable of striking American cities had been discovered in Cuba. He ordered all Russian ships carrying offensive weapons to Cuba to turn back immediately and that "any missile launched from Cuba against the Western Hemisphere would require a full retaliatory response upon the Soviet Union."

Beth was stunned as she and Kenneth stared at each other. "Could this mean that we might go to war with the Soviet Union," Beth asked with concern.

"I believe President Kennedy meant every word he said, so if they don't turn back, it's very possible," Kenneth replied. "We'll just have to wait and see what happens."

Despite tensions being high at school that week and everyone talking about possible war, the Truman High School Rebels won their seventh straight game that Friday night and kept their hopes alive for a city championship.

Thirteen days after Kennedy's television address, Russian ships carrying offensive weapons turned back and the missile bases in Cuba were dismantled.

With the threat of war over, the Truman High School Rebels went on to win their 8th, 9th, and 10th regular season games. For the first time in the history of the school, the Truman Rebels brought home the City Championship Trophy.

Chapter Ten

By 1963, the civil rights movement became more and more violent as African-Americans demanded that action be taken against segregation. By this time, Dr. Martin Luther King, Jr. had become a very well-known activist toward this cause and Beth constantly worried about Eliza Jane and what might happen.

As the middle of April arrived, Beth was looking forward to the end of school. She was so tired of studying, which she doing that night in her room, when she heard the phone ring downstairs.

"Beth, you're wanted on the phone," came Kenneth's voice from the living room. "It's Eliza Jane."

Once downstairs, Beth took the phone from Kenneth. She was glad Eliza Jane had called. It had been several months since they had talked. "Hello, Eliza Jane," she said. "How have you been doing?" she asked.

"I've been fine, Beth. I just wanted you to let you know that I'm going to Birmingham with my brother, Terrance and some of his friends," Eliza Jane began. "Dr. King was arrested and we're going down to join the protest."

"No, no, Eliza Jane, you mustn't go down there," Beth protested emphatically. "It's much, much too dangerous. You could get hurt. Please, please don't go," Beth begged.

"I'm sorry, Beth. I understand your concern, but our plans are already made and we're leaving in the morning," Eliza Jane responded matter-of-factly. "I'll call you when we get home. Bye for now," she added.

Beth said goodbye and hung up the phone. She wished she could have changed Eliza Jane's mind but she knew that she had to fight her own battles and there was nothing she could have said or done that would have made any difference. Birmingham had become the most racially violent city in Alabama. The marches, sit-ins and boycotts had intensified, and Eliza Jane was determined to make this trip.

Later, on television, Beth and her family watched in horror, as news footage showed the demonstrators in Birmingham being blasted with high-pressure water hoses as they marched through Kelly Ingram Park and the city's streets. It made Beth so sad she cried. It was inconceivable to her that people, of any race, could be so cruel.

While getting ready for school the next morning, Beth heard the phone ringing downstairs. After putting on her socks and saddle oxford shoes, she grabbed her books off the bedside table and proceeded down the stairs to the living room. Marie was standing there with a look on her face that made Beth's skin crawl. The first thing that came to her mind was Kenneth. Afraid that he had been in an accident at work, her heart began to race and she put her books down on the coffee table.

"Mama, what's wrong? Has something happened to Kenneth?" she asked as she put her hands on Marie's shoulders and looked deep into her eyes.

"No, sweetheart, it's not Kenneth," Marie replied as she took Beth by the hand. "You'd better come over and sit down on the sofa," she added with unmistakable sadness. "I'm afraid I have some bad news about Eliza Jane."

Beth's heart plummeted and her knees buckled as she fell to the sofa. "What is it, Mama? Did something happen to her in Birmingham? Is she hurt?" Beth asked in desperation.

"That was Eliza Jane's Aunt Cora on the phone just now. You know, she's Mae's sister," Marie continued while Beth continued to get more and more nervous.

"Well, Beth, there is just no easy way to tell you this so I'll just tell you what Cora told me," she added while she continued to hold Beth's hand. "There was an accident last night when Eliza Jane and Terrance were on their way home. According to Terrance, they had stopped for gas just north of Birmingham and it was already dark. After getting back out on the highway, he noticed a car following him real close. He sped up to try and get away but the car came faster and bumped them hard in the rear. They continued bumping into the car until finally Terrance lost control and it ran off the road and flipped several times. He was barely conscious but was able to see several white men standing over them yelling obscenities and telling him that they had gotten what they deserved by coming down there causing trouble.

Beth's heart was racing a mile a minute. "Are they all right, Mama?" she asked. "Is Eliza Jane in the hospital? We need to go see her right away!"

"Beth, honey," Marie said. "Eliza Jane isn't in the hospital. She was thrown from the car and didn't survive."

"Oh, Mama, no. Not Eliza Jane," Beth screamed hysterically as tears streamed down her face and her body shook from her uncontrollable sobs. Marie took her in her arms and tried her best to comfort her. "Beth, I'm so sorry this happened to Eliza Jane. She was such a sweet girt and a good friend to you."

"Mama, she didn't deserved to die just because she wanted to be treated like everyone else. When will people learn to love one another for who they are and stop all the fighting and violence?" Beth asked through tear stained eyes.

"I don't understand it either, Beth, but maybe your generation can make the world a better place for everyone, regardless of color," Marie answered as she lovingly stroked Beth's head.

"You know, Mama, I've already been thinking about this for a long time but now I'm absolutely sure what I want to be when I grow up!" Beth declared.

"What do you want to be, Beth?" Marie asked.

"A Civil Rights lawyer!" Beth answered without reservation.

Chapter Eleven

On September 3, 1963, Beth began her senior year at Truman High School, a day she had looked forward to for many years. However, there would be one difference this year. Northern Alabama had been spared the rioting and violence that had plagued the cities in the south and integration became a reality when a black student was registered at an all-white school in Huntsville, Alabama for the first time.

Beth was extremely happy this Sunday morning as she sat in church thinking about the many things she was grateful for in her life. Two weeks into her senior year and the Rebels had already won their first football game, she had aced every test in every subject so far, Kenneth had gotten a promotion and most of all, Marie seemed to be happier now.

"Mama, how did you like Rev. Henderson's sermon this morning?" Beth asked as she helped her mother finish putting away the dishes after dinner."

"A little boring I thought," Marie answered. "He doesn't have the passion that Rev. Jenkins had that's for sure," she answered with a grin. "He doesn't seem to get the congregation stirred up very much."'

"Hey, you two," yelled Kenneth from the living room. "Come in here!"

Marie and Beth hurried into the living room and were startled at what they saw on the television. All they could do was listen as the newsman described the situation. A bomb had exploded at the Sixteenth Street Baptist Church in Birmingham and four young girls were killed.

Would the violence ever stop, Beth wondered as the three of them sat and watched the gruesome scene.

As Beth got ready for school the next morning her heart went out to the families of the four little girls who were killed in the bombing. She couldn't stop thinking about them, and about Eliza Jane. She knew what she was going to do, and she had to honor Eliza Jane by making things better in the future. It was going to be a busy week, and a busy year, but priority one was keeping up her grades so she could reach her goal.

She was looking forward to all the activities that were planned for the seniors during the coming year. The prom, which she would not attend, was scheduled for mid-April and the class picnic would be held the first weekend in May. Beth was especially looking forward to graduation, which was scheduled for May 29th in the school auditorium. With all of these other activities going on, her focus had to remain on becoming Class Valedictorian, which would not be chosen until the last minute, after the final semester exams.

Friday, November 22, 1963, began just like most other Fridays had at Truman High School and the entire student body was looking forward to another football game and finishing another undefeated season. However, this Friday soon became a Friday like no other.

As Beth sat in her after-lunch study hall, all was quiet when the principal came over the intercom and asked for everyone's attention. She noticed the clock on the wall above the blackboard. It was just past 12:30 in the afternoon. The room became quiet as the class listened. His voice was strained and shaky, giving the class cause for concern. The next words they heard would forever be etched in their memory for they never expected to hear the words they heard at that moment in time.

"It has just been announced on the CBS news that President Kennedy was shot in Dallas, Texas, today during a motorcade through downtown and has been rushed to a nearby hospital. That is all we know at this time but we are monitoring the situation and will keep you informed as soon as we know any more details," the principal announced sadly.

The entire school went silent from shock. You could have heard a pin drop and there was not a dry eye in the entire building. It was inconceivable that anyone would commit such a horrifying act. No one spoke a word for the next twenty-five minutes as they waited quietly for more news. Beth was extremely anxious to hear about the President's condition and couldn't believe that this terrible thing had actually happened. *Who could do such a thing?* she kept asking herself over and over again.

The bell rang at 1:00 for class to change and even the hallway was deathly quiet as the students went to their respective classes. No one was in the mood to study, and the teachers were in no mood to teach. Instead, everyone just sat silently while they anxiously waited for any news about the president.

"May I have your attention please," were the next words they heard once again over the intercom. Beth held her breath and her heart began to pound as she and the rest of the class listened, afraid of what they might hear. "It is with deep sadness that I tell you that President Kennedy has died from his injuries at Parkland Hospital in Dallas."

Tears filled Beth's eyes and she once again looked at the clock above the blackboard. It was just past 1:30 in the afternoon.

That same afternoon, as Air Force One made its way back to Washington D.C., carrying the body of President Kennedy, Vice President Lyndon B. Johnson was sworn in as the new president. A solemn Jackie Kennedy stood next to him in her blood-soaked pink suit.

It was another sad day in the history of the United States, one that would never be forgotten by those who had lived it.

Chapter Twelve

Beth stood silently as she stared into the same old beveled mirror she had stared into as a child. It hung on the wall over the same old tiger oak dresser that had belonged to her grandmother. However, the reflection looking back was not quite the same. That innocent child of long ago had disappeared and here she was wondering about what course the rest of her life would take. It was the night before her high school graduation and all her efforts and hard work had paid off. She had accomplished her goal and was named Class Valedictorian. So why wasn't she happy? She was young and smart and everyone said that she was beautiful.

Only six months and six days had passed since the assassination of President John F. Kennedy in Dallas, an event that had devastated Beth. The more Beth learned about the injustices in the world, the more determined she became. Whatever it took, she was going to become a lawyer, too, just like the Kennedy brothers, Jack and Bobby. She had been offered some small academic scholarships, and they certainly would help, but she would still need more money if she was going to achieve this goal. Her part time job after school at the drug store had helped Kenneth with the household expenses but there wasn't enough for college, too.

In spite of all the bad things that had happened, so many good things had happened in Beth's life, too. She, Roslyn and Richard had spent their high school years together and had swooned away many hours listening to the music of Elvis, Paul Anka, Frankie and

Annette, and Fabian to mention just a few. Now on the scene was this new group from England called the "Beatles." Roslyn thought they were the greatest thing to happen since the invention of lipstick, but Beth wasn't so quick to accept the new group. She would try to keep an open mind, however, for Roslyn's sake. So, all things considered, life was good and she felt very blessed.

"Beth, are you up there?" came Roslyn's loud voice from downstairs.

"I'll be right down, Roz," Beth answered as she finished brushing her long, blonde hair. "Go on in the kitchen and fix us something cold to drink!"

Beth hurried downstairs to find Roslyn sitting at the small kitchen table, sipping on a glass of Coca-Cola and stopped in the doorway. She studied her best friend closely for a moment, remembering that she had always secretly wished that she were more like Roslyn. Her self-confidence overflowed into this bubbly personality that made you feel all warm inside. What other people said or thought didn't bother her at all and she was so beautiful with her dark hair, olive complexion and those gorgeous, jade green eyes. She had an enormous passion for life and a very simple philosophy: live life to the fullest. "If it's fun, and you like it, do it!" she had told Beth many, many times. However, that just wasn't Beth. Beth was too practical and shy, like her mother. She never did things on a whim or just for fun. Besides, she hadn't had much time for fun, especially the last three years.

The boys in mill town had frightened Beth, too. They lived life with a wild abandonment. Nothing mattered to them but having fun, drinking and carousing.

Now, Beth thought as she gathered her nerve, was the time to tell Roslyn of her decision. After much prayer and soul-searching, she had finally decided how she was going to get the money to go to college. Roslyn was not going to like what she was about to hear, so Beth decided to work up to it gradually, hoping that would help soften the surprise and Roslyn's reaction.

"Roz, may I ask you a personal question?" Beth finally asked, as she walked into the kitchen, pulled a chair out from the table and sat down.

"Sure, hon, we've known each other all our lives. You know you can ask me anything," Roslyn replied without hesitation. "But I can't imagine what you could possibly ask me that you don't already know."

Beth swallowed hard, still unsure if she should pursue her planned line of questioning. Knowing Roslyn, she might just knock her out of the chair.

But there was no turning back now. "Have you ever gone all the way?" There she had asked! Now all she had to do was wait for Roslyn's reaction.

Much to Beth's surprise, Roslyn began to laugh hysterically and threw her head back, tossing her dark curls frivolously. However, when she didn't hear Beth join in, her laughter abruptly stopped and she looked Beth straight in the eyes.

"Rachel Elizabeth Benson, I can't believe you are seriously asking me that question!" Roslyn sternly replied after realizing it was no joke.

Beth gathered her wits. She was determined to remain calm and serious as she responded to Roslyn's reaction. "Well, yes, Roz," Beth responded calmly. "I really am seriously asking. Have you ever had s-e-x?"

Roslyn was totally blown away and completely at a loss for words. "You really want to know, don't you?" she asked. But before Beth could answer,

Roslyn put her arms on the table and leaned forward so she could lower her voice. "Well, Beth, it's like this," she began as she looked around the room to make sure no one else was in the kitchen. "Yes, I have," she admitted without hesitation. "As smart as you are, I can't believe you haven't already figured that one out all by yourself," she added as she leaned back in her chair and quietly waited for Beth's reaction.

Beth wasn't really surprised at all and the look on her face told Roslyn so. "I wasn't completely sure, Roz, and it really isn't any of my business but I thought maybe you had with David. You've been going together for a long time," Beth injected with a sigh of relief. "I hope you're not mad at me for asking. I'd never forgive myself if I've hurt your feelings. It's just that you've always been so popular and you always had lots of dates, too, before you met David."

"No, I'm not mad at you for asking, Beth, but I hope you're not implying that that's the only reason the boys were going out with me instead of you!" Roslyn answered back somewhat upset at the implication she thought Beth was making.

Beth sensed Roslyn's hurt and immediately apologized. "No! No! Roz, believe me. I didn't mean it that way at all. I'm sorry if I made it sound that way. Please forgive me," Beth assured as she leaned across the table and put her hand on Roslyn's arm. "You're so beautiful and you're so much fun to be with. You're everything I'm not. Why wouldn't the boys want to date you instead of me?"

Now Roslyn felt like apologizing to Beth. "I'm sorry, too, Beth. I know you didn't mean it that way," she said. "You were right, too, about David. He was my first, and he's been my only one," she explained. "And for your information, all the boys **did** want to date you but they were just afraid to ask," Roslyn added with great conviction.

"Afraid? Why would they have been afraid?" Beth asked somewhat confused at this newfound information.

"Because they were afraid of being turned down. Whether you think so or not, Beth, you are very beautiful. Maybe they were intimidated because you are so beautiful and smart, too!" Roslyn answered.

"It's just as well," Beth replied. "I probably wouldn't have gone out with any of them anyway. Besides, I've never thought of myself as being pretty. You know that," Beth said as she intently studied Roslyn's face. "If I asked you another question, would you promise to tell me the truth?"

"Of course I will. We definitely have no secrets now," Roslyn answered. "What is it?" she asked as she took a sip of coke from her glass.

Beth gathered her nerves once again before asking the question. "Do you think . . . a man would . . . want me . . . that way?" Beth asked stuttering and nervously rubbing her hands together.

Roslyn was totally confused at Beth's question. "What in the world are you getting at? I just told you that you are very beautiful. Someday, when you least expect it, a gorgeous "hunk" is going to fall head-over-heals in love with you and you with him," Roslyn replied adamantly. "Are you afraid you're going to be a virgin all your life? Is that what all these questions are about?" she asked with wide-eyed curiosity.

"No, that's not what I'm afraid of and that's not what I meant by my question," Beth said as she got up and got another tray of ice from the freezer. It sure was hot tonight, she thought, as she filled their glasses with more ice and coke. How could she make Roslyn understand what she meant without saying the word, 'prostitute.' "This is what I want to know, Roz," she began slowly. "Do you think a man would **pay** to be with me without being in love with me?" Beth asked as she filled the ice trays and put them back in the freezer. There was only silence as she walked over and sat back down at the table. Slowly, she sat Roslyn's glass down in front of her and waited patiently for some sort of reaction from her.

Roslyn had been waiting patiently, too, for Beth to clarify her question but her answer was totally unexpected and unbelievable. Shock wouldn't begin to describe what she was feeling at this moment. She was mortified at the obvious meaning of what Beth had said and was determined to find out just exactly what was going on in her mind. Just as she was about to pursue her investigation into the subject matter, Richard suddenly appeared at the back door.

"What's up?" he asked, a big grin on his face as he opened the screened door and walked into the kitchen. "Talking about graduation?"

"Hardly!" Roslyn replied with a huff, all the while giving Beth a look that would kill the already dead. "You're not going to believe what our Beth has on her mind!" she added, pointing furiously at her own head.

"Whatever it is, it sure has gotten your dandruff up, sis. I can sure tell that," Richard exclaimed as he leaned his tall, lanky body up against the sink and crossed his arms over his wide, muscular chest.

Suddenly, Roslyn stood up and pushed her chair back with such furry that it turned over and crashed against the tile floor. Choosing to simply ignore it, she walked over to Richard and studied his face intently for a moment. He would probably want to strangle Beth when he found out what she was planning, Roslyn thought, as she prepared to tell Richard Beth's plan.

"I can tell you this, dear brother, it's going to get your dandruff up, too, when you hear what I just heard," Roslyn began in a heated voice. "I guess it's a good thing you came over here tonight because we've got a big, big problem. You know how much Beth wants to go to college and become a lawyer, right?" Roslyn asked.

"Yes, I do," Richard complied with a nod.

"Well, I just found out how she plans to earn the money. She's going to . . . ," Roslyn began but was quickly interrupted by Beth.

"Roz, I can tell Richard myself," Beth exclaimed. She had been quietly listening to Roslyn but could no longer remain silent. Getting up from her chair a little more ladylike than Roslyn had, she slowly walked over and stood beside the two best friends she had in the world. "Besides, Richard plays a huge part in my decision, so I should be the one to tell him my plan," she confessed.

There was one hundred percent pure confusion in Richard's eyes as Beth studied this face she knew so well. He had grown into a tall, extremely handsome young man with a wide, beautiful smile. Being an All-Star basketball player all through high school had also made him extremely popular with all the girls. That's why Beth knew he would be very experienced at what she needed and wanted him to do.

Finally, after what seemed like an eternity, Beth took a deep breath for courage and began to tell Richard her plan. "This is what I've decided to do. I'm going to use the best resource I have at my disposal to make money for college. It will take less time than any other part time job that I can think of, time that I can spend studying, and I can make much more money, too," she concluded with certainty.

"I'd love to have a job like that, Beth," Richard said, rubbing his hands together in anticipation of finding out what it was. "Delivering groceries for Mr. Stiles is hard work and it sure doesn't pay much. Just tell me what I have to do and I'll join you!" he added with excitement.

Obviously, Richard wasn't as quick as Roslyn at figuring out some things.

"No you wouldn't!" exclaimed Roslyn. "Believe me you wouldn't," she added as she picked her chair up off the floor and sat it upright again. Thoroughly disgusted with Beth, she sat back down and began tapping her fingers on the table. She had to think of something, anything, to say that would change Beth's mind. "Just wait until you hear the rest of the story," she added looking at Richard, her jade green eyes shooting sparks.

"O.K., Beth, I'm waiting," Richard said, taking a more serious attitude with his arms still folded across his chest. "This plan of yours seems to have Roslyn more than just a little upset, so you'd better tell me exactly what it is you're talking about."

Beth was suddenly gripped with fear. Richard had always acted like "another big brother" where she was concerned by always trying to protect her. Because of that, she knew he would try to change her mind, especially when he found out what part she wanted him to play in her decision. Her heart began to palpitate and before she began, she took one last deep breath for good measure. "I'm going to use my body!" she blurted out. "It's as simple as that!" she added matter-of-factly, putting her hands on her hips as a sign of determination. She thought that gesture might help her case.

Richard gasped in horrified disbelief. Without hesitation, he grabbed Beth by the shoulders and looked into those sapphire blue eyes. It was all he could do to keep from shaking her senseless. *What is happening? What are you thinking?* Richard thought. "You're going to do what?" he screamed. "No way in hell! You can just forget that idea right here and now because I forbid it, Beth! I won't let you do it!" he protested adamantly.

Beth wasn't shaken by Richard's reaction because she knew exactly what it would be and she had prepared herself. "You're not only going to let me, Richard, but you're going to help me," she declared with a calmness that sent a cold chill over Richard as if ice water were running through his veins.

Roslyn was dumbfounded at what she had just heard and sat motionless at the table looking at Beth in total disbelief and confusion.

Richard was in even worse shape than Roslyn as he wondered just what part he could possibly play in Beth's plan. "And just how, I'd like to know, am I supposed to help you do such a crazy, stupid thing?" Richard questioned. "Beth, I believe you've totally lost your mind!" he declared as he looked at Roslyn and shook his head in complete and utter disbelief.

"No, I haven't lost my mind, so just listen to what I have to say, please," Beth begged. "You know that I've never been with a boy before, Richard, and I'd . . . well, I'd like for you to be my first," she added as she deliberately avoided eye contact with him.

"Roslyn!" Richard yelled as he flung his arms about wildly and walked around and around the table. "Did you hear that? Have you ever heard such nonsense in your entire life?" he ranted. "Not only does Beth want to become a prostitute, she wants **ME** to be the one to take her virginity! I can't believe it! I must be in some kind of damn nightmare or something. Hello! Somebody wake me the hell up!" he ranted furiously.

This last development was as much of a surprise to Roslyn as it was to Richard. "It's no nightmare, believe me," said Roslyn. "But I know one thing for sure. If we don't talk her out of this, it will become a nightmare and we'll all be in it for the rest of our lives!"

Richard slowly took Beth in his arms and held her close to him. She could feel his heart beating furiously in his chest. She knew he was very upset with her but she had to stand her ground. This is what she had to do and she wasn't going to let him or Roslyn change her mind.

After a long silence, Richard finally spoke. "Beth, we've known each other our entire lives and you know that I love you the same way I love Roslyn. That's why you can't ask me to make love to you," he pleaded. "I just can't do it, so there's nothing else left to say on the subject. We'll just have to think of another way for you to get the money for college. We'll just have to," he insisted. "That's all there is to it!"

"There is no other way!" Beth exclaimed. "Don't you think I've tried to think of another way? I don't want to do this, but Kenneth works all the time and Mama takes in sewing and ironing and we still barely make ends meet," Beth argued determined not to give up. "You both know that I've had my heart set on becoming a lawyer for a long time and that's exactly what I intend to do, with or without your help! My mind is made up and there's nothing either of you can say that will change it. So, I would appreciate your **HELP** instead. Richard, are you going to be my first, or will it be some stranger who doesn't care?" Beth asked once again putting Richard on the spot.

Richard didn't know what to say. What else could he say? Beth seemed determined to go through with this ridiculous "plan" of hers regardless of his and Roslyn's protests.

"Have you really thought this through completely, Beth? How are you going to fool your mother? What are you going to do after you finish college? What's going to happen when you meet someone and fall in love? What are you going to tell him? Have you thought about any of this?" Roslyn asked throwing question after question at Beth. "This just can't be happening!" she gasped with a sigh of defeat.

Even Roslyn's bombardment of questions didn't deter Beth. "I have it all worked out, you two," Beth assured. "I'll tell Mama that I have a job at night and I'll need the truck. Kenneth usually goes to bed right after supper anyway. I can ride the bus to school during the day when Kenneth needs the truck. I'll have to leave every night so Mama won't get suspicious, but I won't have to work every night," Beth explained. "You see, on the nights I don't have to work, I'll go to the library and study instead. When I'm working, I'll go into Dexter where no one knows me. This way I'll have enough money for school and I'll also have plenty of time to study. Only the three of us will ever know," she said confident that her plan would work.

A sincere sadness came over Roslyn and Richard as they finally realized that all their efforts to change Beth's mind were in vain. They were defeated. Both looked as though they had just lost their best friend as they listened to Beth's ridiculous and self-destructive plan.

"Hey, you two, don't look so gloomy," Beth scorned trying to lift their spirits. "I'm only going to do this for two years. I'll get my associate's degree and become a paralegal. This will get me a good job in a law firm. Once I have a job, I can go to school at night and work on my law degree. And as for falling in love, Roz, that's not in my plan at all," Beth concluded.

"Beth, you may think you have everything under control, but things don't always happen exactly the way we want them to," Roslyn tried to explain. "Kenneth could find out somehow and it would hurt him terribly. And don't say you're not going to fall in love because you can't predict that either!" she added continuing her argument against Beth's plan.

"Roz, I have to take the risk," Beth said firmly once again. "There's just no other way to get what I want!"

"What a tangled web we weave, when first we practice to deceive," quoted Roslyn from behind sad eyes. "Just remember that."

"That sounds just like something Mama would say," replied Beth harshly. "I'm not going to be hurting anyone except myself and I'll have to live with it, not you," she retorted, pointing at Roslyn, "so don't you worry about it."

Richard had listened to this conversation long enough and had had all he could take. He still couldn't believe that Beth was actually going to go through with this plan of hers. He only knew that he couldn't be a part of it. "I'm sorry, Beth, but I just can't do this," he said shaking his hanging head. "I can't help you ruin your life! I just couldn't live with myself if I did," he added as he turned and stalked out of the kitchen, letting the screen door slam shut behind him.

Beth quickly followed Richard into the small backyard and caught him by the arm. She didn't want him to leave upset but she had no any idea what she could say to change his mind. "Richard, please don't leave yet. Come over here and let's sit in the swing," she pleaded not ready to give up on him just yet.

Richard nodded in agreement and quietly followed Beth over and sat down beside her in the swing that hung from a large branch on the huge oak tree in the yard. The full moon was a glimmering, bright-white ball against the black, starlit sky and a soft, warm breeze was gently teasing the leaves on the tree. Only the sound of chirping crickets and other creatures of the night filled the otherwise quiet May night.

Beth looked into Richard's sad eyes and then took his hand and softly placed it in hers. Her heart ached and he looked so hurt and confused. "Richard, I really need for you to understand how I feel. This isn't easy for me either but that doesn't bother me. I'll get through this and then I'll get over it. So will you and Roz and life will go on, I promise," Beth continued hoping to somehow convince Richard. "What does bother me is having a total stranger be the first man to ever make love to me. I want with all my heart for my first time to be with you. Can't you understand why?" Beth asked.

"I don't understand any of this, Beth," Richard answered as he lovingly squeezed her hand while tears gathered in his eyes.

"Richard, you know that I would never even consider doing such a thing if I didn't need the money so desperately. It's my only chance to get out of mill town and have the kind of life I've always dreamed of for as long as I can remember," Beth added as she squeezed his hand in return. "If I don't do this, I'll be working in that mill for the rest of my life, just like everyone else, with no future whatsoever. I've made up my mind and there's nothing you or Roz can say that will change it. So please, Richard, I'm begging you. Won't you at least think about it some more before you say no?" Beth pleaded as tears filled her eyes, too.

Richard sat motionless for a long time, staring out into the darkness. What was he to do? Beth meant so much to him. More than she knew. How could he let some stranger who didn't care about her take her innocence and have it mean nothing? He didn't think he could let that happen. Neither did he think he could do what she was asking. He turned and looked at Beth sitting there next to him. She was so young and naïve, and with the moonlight shinning on her flawless complexion, she was more beautiful than ever. He could see the tears glistening in her blue eyes. She was nothing like the other girls he had been with. Right now he just wanted to take her in his arms and hold her and magically make everything all right. But he couldn't. His stomach was churning and he felt as though he would be sick. Beth was waiting, but he had no answer for her tonight.

Gathering his courage, he finally spoke. "I'm sorry, Beth, but I can't give you an answer tonight. You've really put a heavy burden on my heart and I have to give this some serious thought. I'll give you fair warning, though, I plan to keep on trying to change your mind, whatever my decision is. I'll let you know tomorrow night after graduation," he said as he slowly stood up and started walking away. "Would you please tell Roslyn that I've gone home?" He asked.

"Of course," Beth answered as she watched him disappear around the corner of the house. She hated to put pressure on him but she wanted him, and only him, to be her first. She knew he would be kind and gentle because he cared for her. However, if he did say "no", it wouldn't change her mind. She had already set the wheels in motion by seeing a doctor in Dexter two months ago for birth control pills. There was no turning back now.

Chapter Thirteen

With the graduation ceremonies only an hour away, Beth was a bundle of nerves. Not only was Richard going to give her his answer tonight, being Class Valedictorian brought with it the responsibility of giving a speech. She wasn't looking forward to that part of the evening in the least. She had been practicing in front of the mirror all week, but for the first time, as she stood looking at herself in her white cap and gown, it all seemed so real and final. A part of her life would be over after tonight and she could never get it back. Her life would never be the same again.

Whether or not Richard agreed to what she wanted, she had paved the road to her future and all she had to do now was start her journey. Picking up the brush from the dresser, she gave her long, shimmering blonde hair one last stroke then hurried downstairs where Kenneth and Marie were waiting.

The ceremony only took a couple of hours and Beth's speech "brought down the house." Richard found Beth outside the gymnasium afterwards surrounded by her loving family. They were extremely proud of her tonight. *What would they say if they knew what she was planning?* Richard thought as he quietly watched the display of affection taking place before him. He could just see it all now. Kenneth would go into an unbridled rage and lock Beth in the house indefinitely and her mother would start sobbing uncontrollably. Not a pretty scene at all and certainly not one that Richard would want to witness.

"That was one great speech, Beth," Richard interrupted, giving her a big bear hug. "You have every reason to be proud of yourself."

"Thank you. You're very sweet to say that," Beth replied a little embarrassed.

"I wasn't saying it to be sweet," Richard replied. "It's the truth. Isn't that right, Kenneth?" he asked giving Kenneth a slap on the shoulder.

"You bet! She's the greatest. Mama and I couldn't be prouder of our little girl!" Kenneth declared happily.

"I wish you all would stop!" Beth begged with a laugh. "You're embarrassing me."

"O.K. then, I'll change the subject," Richard said looking at Beth. "Are you going to any of the post graduation parties tonight?"

"No, I didn't make any plans. Roz and David asked me if I wanted to make the rounds with them to all the different parties but they don't need me tagging along ruining their fun. Guess I'll just go home with Mama and Kenneth," Beth answered while searching Richard's face for some clue as to whether or not he had made a decision concerning her earlier request.

Richard wasn't stupid. He could read the questioning look in Beth's eyes, but the only real decision he had made was to keep trying to change her mind. "Would you like to go to Shorty's with me for a hamburger and a root beer?" he asked.

The mere mention of food reminded Beth that she had not eaten all day and she suddenly realized that she was actually very hungry. But could she eat? She was so nervous about what Richard's answer was going to be she didn't know if she could put anything in her stomach. Regardless of whether or not she could eat, she had to go to find out his answer.

"Sure," she answered, "If it's all right with you and Mama," she said to Kenneth.

Kenneth knew they wanted to go out and have some fun. He wasn't too old to remember his high school graduation night. After all, it had only been eight years ago. "Of course it's all right, squirt," he answered with a grin. "You two go on and have fun. I'll take Mama home. We're both tired anyway and we'll see you tomorrow," he added as he put his arm around Marie's shoulder and gave her a hug.

Beth removed her gown that she wore over a white dress and gave it and her cap to Marie to take home.

"Goodnight, honey," Marie said as she gave Beth a kiss on the cheek. "Don't be out too late though. You know what they say, nothing good happens after midnight."

"I won't, Mama," Beth promised as she watched them walk off toward the truck. She prayed with all her heart that they would never find out what she was going to do. She knew how terribly hurt they would be and would probably never forgive her. That's why she would have to do everything in her power to make sure they never found out.

Richard grabbed Beth by the hand and they ran for the parking lot where he had parked his old jalopy of a car, of which he was very proud. He had practically built it from the ground up with old spare parts. Once they reached the car, Richard removed his gown and threw it and his cap in the back seat, then slung his long legs over the side of the car and slid down under the steering wheel. It had no top, which made Beth extremely grateful that it was not raining. She decided, however, to open the door instead of doing the high jump into the seat.

"I'm sorry I didn't get the door for you, Beth," Richard apologized. "I'm just so used to getting in this way I didn't even think."

"That's all right," Beth insisted with a laugh. "You don't have to treat me like you would a real date, you know."

"But you are a real date," he declared as he started the car still sorry he hadn't opened the door for her.

Neither one said a word during the ride to Shorty's. Beth could only wonder what was going through Richard's mind. Was he or wasn't he going to say **yes**. The thought of some strange man callously and thoughtlessly taking her for the first time made her blood run ice cold. She had always thought that her first time would be with the man she loved but life had not provided her with that opportunity. Now, she looked to Richard, the best and dearest friend she had ever had.

The ride to Shorty's didn't take long and Richard turned the car into the lot and parked at one of the drive-up speakers. Soon their order for burgers was placed and he looked over at Beth nervously sitting next to him. For the first time in his life he felt uneasy with her and he didn't much like the feeling. He had to think of something to say that would change her mind. But what could it be. He had tried everything he knew to say or do. Maybe some reverse psychology would work. At this point in time, anything was worth a try.

"Beth . . . about what you want me to do," he began slowly. "I've thought about nothing else since last night and I've made a decision," he said after clearing the frog that had suddenly appeared in his throat. "Since you're dead set on going through with this crazy idea of yours, you don't give me much choice. I care about you and I just can't and won't let your first experience be with a total stranger. I'll be your first, but only for your sake. You know that I'm still one hundred percent against what you're doing, don't you?" he asked, looking into her exquisite blue eyes. He knew he would have no problem making love to Beth. After all, he was a man and what man in his right mind would? But he was genuinely concerned about how this was going to affect her and their relationship.

All of the fear and anxiety vanished when Beth heard Richard's words. That was all that she wanted to hear. Without thinking, she leaned over and gave him a big hug and kissed him gently on the cheek.

Much to his surprise, Richard found himself physically excited by Beth's response. *Must be all this talk about sex,* he thought, as he gently pushed her away, still confused by his unexpected arousal.

"What's wrong," asked Beth, surprised at Richard's reaction.

Awkwardly trying to gain control of the situation, he blurted out like a child whose hand had just been caught in the cookie jar, "Nothing's wrong, Beth. I just didn't mean right now, right here in the car!" he declared somewhat caught off guard by his reaction. He had hugged Beth hundreds of times. Why was this time so different? He had hoped, however, that she would back out when he agreed to go along with her idea, but she hadn't. Now what was he going to do?

"I know that," Beth replied, a little peeved at him for thinking that she would even think such a thing. "Have you decided where and when yet?"

Richard was paying the carhop, who had just placed the tray of food on the window. He handed

Beth her hamburger and root beer while he tried to think of an answer to her question. All he could think of was to put the ball back in her court. "That's up to you, Beth. This whole thing is your idea, not mine," he replied before taking a bite of his hamburger.

"As soon as possible is fine with me," she answered. "The sooner I get past this, the more relaxed I'll be and I can get on with what I have to do. I'll have all summer to make some money before classes start in the fall," she added. "Now let's eat these burgers before they get cold."

Richard looked at Beth in awe, completely astonished at her calm demeanor. This simply wasn't the Beth he had known all his life. "I still can't believe you're actually going to go through with this! Have you even given any thought to birth control?" he asked, hoping for a way to stall her.

"Oh, yes!" Beth exclaimed her mouth full of burger. "I've been taking birth control pills for two months now."

Richard was speechless and his churning stomach made it difficult for him to keep his burger down. It seemed as if there was nothing he could say or do to change her mind. She had called his bluff and he had lost. When they were finished eating, he placed their glasses on the tray and beeped the horn for the carhop. Dangling his hands over the steering wheel, he sighed, feeling hopelessly caught, as if in a spider web, in Beth's plan. On second thought, maybe he could scare her by suggesting that they get it over with right now, tonight.

"Very well, Beth, if we're really going to do this thing, I guess tonight is as good a time as any," he said as he reached down and started the engine. As he backed the car out and pulled out into the street, he waited for Beth to say something but there was only silence. "I'll find a nice motel and we'll get this over with ASAP," he added with a taste of sarcasm hoping Beth would back out at the last minute.

At first Beth was surprised at Richard's sudden gung-ho attitude until she realized what he was trying to do. It wasn't going to work though. She sat quietly and made no attempt to stop him. Besides, the wind felt cool and refreshing blowing through her hair and against her face.

Richard's eyes left the road only long enough to take a quick glance at Beth. He was praying, harder than he ever had in his entire life, she would back down but he could see that it wasn't going to happen. He could tell by the look on her face that his plan had backfired. This was actually going to happen so he might as well accept it.

"Whatever you say is fine with me, Richard," Beth finally said.

Richard's heart skipped a beat. He believed that he was more scared than Beth and he had had more than his share of "experiences." Of course, none of them had been with Beth, or anyone like Beth, and there was a definite difference. He hadn't cared for any of the others the way he cared for Beth.

"This one is nice," he said as he turned the car into the first motel he came to and parked in front of the office. "You wait here and I'll be right back. I hope he doesn't ask for our marriage license."

As she waited, Beth tried to talk herself out of what she was about to do, but she only became more and more determined. It was the only way. She was afraid, no doubt about it. But she knew she could trust Richard, so she took a deep breath and mentally prepared herself. Her thoughts were interrupted when Richard jumped back into the car.

"All set," he said as he started the car. "The guy didn't even ask for a marriage license."

Slowly, Richard drove around to the back of the motel and parked in front of one of the rooms. Putting his arm across the back of the seat, he turned to look at Beth. He had to try one more time. "I can still take you home, Beth," he pleaded. "It's not too late to forget this crazy plan of yours."

"Yes it is. There's no turning back now," Beth said as she opened the car door, got out and walked to the door of the room. Frozen with fear, she waited for Richard to unlock the door.

Richard turned off the engine and followed Beth to the door. His hand was trembling as he tried to put the key in the lock. Beth steadied his hand and the door opened. Once inside, he immediately began checking out the T.V., the lights and anything else he could use as a stalling device, ignoring Beth completely. She knew exactly what he was doing and she understood. She was scared, too, but someone had to make the first move, and it looked like it was going to have to be her.

"Richard, come here," Beth said holding out her hand. He walked over and stood in front of her, taking her hand in his. When she looked deep into his eyes, all his fears disappeared and she pulled him close to her and whispered in his ear. "I don't know what to do, so, please, I'm depending on you to show me."

Richard was truly unable to resist any longer as Beth innocently offered herself to him. He slowly lowered his head and delicately kissed her waiting lips. Putting his arm around her tiny waist, he pulled her even closer to him. Beth returned his kiss as fear completely engulfed her trembling body.

Being young and hot blooded, Richard's desire quickly heightened. *This is Beth! How can I be doing this?* he thought to himself. However, he was, and the last thing he wanted to do was rush her so he had to remember to keep it slow. With that in mind, his shaking hands began to slowly unbutton her dress. Beth shivered at his touch and he stopped. "Are you sure?" he asked. She nodded and closed her eyes. Her dress fell to the floor, and he gently picked her up in his arms and carried her to the bed. Richard undressed in the darkness and lay down beside her.

"It's still not too late to change your mind, Beth," he whispered as he propped himself up on his elbow and stroked a lock of hair away from her face. "I'm not even sure if I can go through with this myself.

You know I wouldn't hurt you for the world, Beth, but I've never been with a virgin," he added.

Beth didn't speak. Instead, she rolled toward him and put her arm across his chest. "I know you wouldn't hurt me. Don't worry," she whispered.

Richard kissed her lovingly, as though she were a fragile flower whose delicate petals would fall off if touched too harshly. There, in the dark, a sleeping passion awoke between them and Beth began the journey that would determine the rest of her life. It didn't matter that she would have to lie to her family. It didn't matter that she would have to become this other person. It didn't matter that she was using her best friend to help her accomplish her goal. The decision had been made to lay the foundation on which to build her future and for now, that was all that mattered.

The End

Book II in the *Happy Birthday, Beth* series . . .

"The Deception"

It is June, 1966, one month before Beth's 20th birthday. Beth is a recent graduate of Dunbar Community College, where she received her Associate's Degree in Paralegal Studies. She continues the pursuit of her goal to become a lawyer after being hired by a prestigious law firm. While working for the firm, her earlier decisions come back to haunt her, threatening the life she has built for herself and her hopes for the future. After Beth buries her husband who is killed in action in Vietnam, the deception must continue.

Please visit www.LBBradyBooks.com for ordering information.

www.ingramcontent.com/pod-product-compliance
Lightning Source LLC
Chambersburg PA
CBHW050028180626
46810CB00002B/625